CONSTELIS VOL. 2

CONSTELIS VOL. 2

PATTERN RECOGNITION

K. LEIGH

k. LEIGH

This is a work of fiction. Names, characters, places, and incidents either are the product of the author's imagination or are used fictitiously. Any resemblance to actual persons, living or dead, events, or locales is entirely coincidental.

Editing by Madalyn Rupprecht
Book design by L. Austen Johnson
Editing and formatting facilitated by Dr. Rissy's Writing & Marketing
Cover Art by Kira Leigh Maintanis

ISBN: 978-1-7368053-1-2 (paperback)
ASIN: B08X7KN68L (ebook)

https://constelisvoss.ml

k. LEIGH

CONTENTS

Content Warning:

The following story contains abuse, trauma, PTSD, sexual assault, bigotry, and explicit violence. It is not a piece of fiction that engenders contemporary realities gently, including marginalized identities such as sex workers, LGBTQIAA+ individuals, and people of color.

Please consider this your warning for a work of fiction, which exists as a metacritique of the politics of power told through a space opera through one vector of a reality painted dystopic.

I ask only one thing of you, should you find yourself skimming its pages—enter this self-aware living landscape and question everything.

I hope it teaches who it must, and comforts those I wish to reach. I aim to let my readers know I see them in all their complicated inner paintings.

Good luck, and know that I love you desperately.

THE PATTERN

"As far back as I can remember myself—and I remember myself with lawless lucidity, I have been my own accomplice, who knows too much, and therefore is dangerous."

— Vladimir Nabokov: "Invitation to a Beheading".
Sovremennye zapiski, 1935

V

"When someone shows you who they are, believe them the first time."

— *Maya Angelou*

That's an old quote I've grown fond of in my even older age, because the truth it speaks will never be unmade.

I like to think I've listened plenty of times, but perhaps I only heard what I wanted to hear, hoping someone would give me 'something awesome', despite knowing they're incapable.

Humans have this amazing capacity to delude themselves. They can love someone who is absolute shit to them, and have no awareness of just how horrible they are, even when brought face to face with the true colors of the one they love.

They can also repeatedly hurt themselves, over and over again, and move in the same exact cycles of abuse they try to escape, even when they tell themselves to stop.

Even when everyone around them is telling them to stop, they just can't listen.

Remember, I'm crazy, not stupid. I listen, but...can I learn?

Can *we* learn?

It's been repeatedly proven that every version of myself defaults to cycles of abuse, war, trauma, and death when shit hits the fan.

It's been repeatedly proven that people never learn, and always end up fighting a fucking war of ideals in the sky, with clouds between their thighs.

Even if I wrote the script—and I hope beyond all hopes that enough variables step outside my parameters to defeat the GIGO principle I'm still yet fighting—it never changes.

It just delays the inevitable. Because nobody truly listens, and worse yet, they don't fucking learn.

So, for every block of color you've seen, I hope you listened to what it told you. And for every repetition, errant object, and flickering inconsistency, I hope you'll find the pattern.

Because there's going to come a moment in this play where you have to truly listen. Depending on what you hear, you'll have a choice to make in how you interpret it, and therefore, what you learn and think of me.

It is not simple, nor is it easy.

But if you wanted easy, you'd have never opened this haunted fucking file to begin with.

ALEX DESCENDED via the elevator to where he knew Diana worked. From his mouth streamed smoke in a river of payne's gray. This was his element. This was who he was. This was what he was meant to do.

This was his pattern, his prime directive, his job, his repetition.

The walls around him trapped smoke, the atmospheric system halting and sputtering to work overtime to remove this illegal substance. He glared as he fell down each floor, the rushing of the elevator painting feathers of colors over his face.

Al lifted up his shirt, the cigarette dusting ash on it. He tapped his chest compartment and removed a gun. A very real, gunpowder and metal, gun.

Compartment back in place, shirt down, he ran his fingers through his hair and paused for a moment. As the elevator came to a stop, he primed his weapon. The black metal felt heavy and good in his hand.

The doors opened, and he stalked onto the floor, leading with his squared shoulders. A guard approached, and he shot him through the face. Blood splattered onto a clear desk behind him. The man fell like a stone, his brain matter cast off on the wall like a painting.

He heard a scream.

Alex picked up the guard's laser rifle and pointed it forty-five degrees, and shot another guard straight through his left eye. The man was down, his eye socket blown straight through, flesh singed on the edges like a cigarette burn.

More rushed in, and Alex shot them. He stepped over their bodies to create more corpses with more bullets. When the bullets wouldn't suffice, lasers. When fists were more effective, fists.

A well-placed laser blew a searing hole through a secretary's core. Needless collateral damage, but he made it a point to blow her up all over her transparent computer terminal.

This violence would be his new calling card; no more little birds on slips of paper left as a warning. The blood would be the rosed lips—no paint necessary. These thoughts came to him like drowning, flickering images once-lived, now-remembered, now-relived in metal, and impossible energy.

Cigarette between his lips, clenched in the teeth, Alex took out another desk worker because he quite simply could. The entire time he wore a mute smile, but soon it became an appetizing expression as blood painted Judicial in rivers of red.

More bodies dropped. Alex's smile never did.

BEFORE THE WAR MACHINE, the guns, and the girl with hair like the sun, Henry had lived a simple life. He spent his days shoveling, fixing atmospheric systems, building, and working with his hands.

Henry had been a worker and seemingly, had wished for nothing more than to do just that.

Looks, however, always deceived. There had come a day when he'd wished for more, and on that day, he'd found his answer without actually hearing it.

On this day, Henry looked like he smelled. He surely smelled worse than he looked. Henry looked at the earth he was digging up and chewed a piece of grass between his lips.

An older woman had come by with a bucket of water on her head. She balanced it with her other hand and picked up her dress to traverse the shifting earth. She was dressed in purple robes, dyed from the flowers that grew in abundance all over The Greens.

"Son. What's with the frown?" the older woman asked with a graveled voice.

"I dunno' gran...I'm missin' somethin'," Henry replied, striking the dirt with his shovel.

"Missin'? What's there to miss?" She inhaled the crisp air into her lungs and set down her water bucket on soft earth.

"Green grass, clean air, running water. Plenty o' food. Better than some'o the others. You should be grateful."

"Yeah, yeah gran...I'm grateful awright..." Henry spit out the grass in his mouth and went back to digging. The hot sun shone down and made his work all that much harder.

The old woman took a sip of water from her bucket with a ladle and offered him some with a gesture. Henry walked beside her, stooped to drink, and a voice called out.

"Fix it!"

Startled, Henry spilled water all down his blue shirt. The old woman scolded him. When he blinked down at the ladle and the water on his shirt, the familiar sage color resumed. No blue.

"Mind's playin' tricks on me," he said with a chuckle, going back for another deep sip of cool water.

"Hmm?"

"Nothin', gran."

POLLY, in our present time, was staring at Henry as though he'd grown another head.

"Earth to Henry! Helllooo? Can you help me get my coat or whatever? I'm soaked through..."

Polly dredged herself out of the water, and Henry followed after, stomping through the mud. Polly wrung the water out of her thin white slip, droplets falling on the grass.

A bug flew by his head, and he swatted at it with a

grimace. Now preoccupied with the insect trying to attack him, he'd forgotten what she asked.

"Henry."

"Oh, oh. Roight, roight." Henry grabbed Polly's lab coat and stretched it out to her like an offering.

"We should get going. They're, like, probably waiting for us...Can you walk with me?"

Polly's question knocked Henry back to reality. He hesitated; his dark brows were thick lines in mottled ink. They dropped as she stepped closer.

"Pardon?" Henry stammered.

"I hurt my leg a little bit, and my shoes are dirty or whatever."

"Yeah, sure, Poll. Sure."

The sun pulled the moisture from their clothes as the pair walked. Side by side, through the wheat field, through the ruddy pathway Polly had mowed down. She shifted as they walked, her leg tender, but it wasn't that bad.

"Your...hair," Henry tried to form cogent words, which seemed a feat for the tall man.

"My hair? What about my hair? Is it, like, gross?" Polly pulled at the wet blonde strands hanging over her face and tried to find bug, brush, or beast. She found nothing and pouted at him, fingers tangled up in the strands of yellow knots.

"It's...gold 'n all that. Like the...yeah. And the..." Henry pointed at the sky.

"What a way with words you have, Henry..." Polly rolled her eyes and then shot him a cheeky grin. She started to laugh and then snorted.

"The fuck was that, mate?"

"S-sorry? I snorted...you know..."

"Thought Maya was the piglet," Henry said as he cracked an awkward smile.

"Y-you're the pig!"

Polly pushed Henry with her shoulder. He chuckled and pushed back. The two leaned on each other as they walked. Then their hands found themselves dangling uselessly.

Polly's gentle, thin pinky extended out to brush against his own. His skin was warm and rough. Hers was cold and fair.

"Brave girl, eh?" Their linked fingers were impossibly protective of their tender hearts. Every movement was a risk; the carefulness said as much.

"Ah, fack! We left tha rest of ya clothes back at th' river!" He was far more distraught than she was. Their hands fell from one another.

"It's alright. I have more clothes in my 'cell', or whatever."

"You don't want jus one'o 'em? Like, shoes?" Henry stopped walking, but Polly continued. He pulled her back with his hand, fingers together in his own, in softness.

"One shoe?" she asked, brow raised.

"No, I mean…"

"That's…the old me…I don't want to be that anymore," she said.

"I want to be myself." Polly pulled him forward, and Henry reluctantly followed. He watched the back of her head bob with every footstep.

"I want to do what I want. I don't want rules. Just like he has no rules," she continued.

Henry looked down at his feet. Polly's words sounded familiar; poetry from another time.

"I dunno what yer on about, Poll. Waddaya mean?"

Henry dragged his vision back up to Polly's head; the sun was flicked off. Under a black sky, Polly continued to walk. Henry continued to follow.

Soon, the buzzing insects were deleted from view. The golden wheat around them swept away. The earth beneath their feet evaporated. With each step, another thing disappeared, until it was Polly's turn to vanish.

In her place was another hand—Alex's—and with just one tug, Henry was ripped from The Greens altogether.

HENRY WAS in a place filled with flashing lights. Gone was the field of wheat, the bugs, the brush, the warm soil, the jutting rocks, the flowers, the birds. Gone was Polly and her golden hair. Gone was the blue sky. Everything was dark, and then the lights burned into view.

It was bright, and there were loud noises. He heard music—music he shouldn't have known but did.

A woman beside him laughed hysterically, drowning much of it out. He squinted as if squinting would help turn up the volume of the song.

"Billy Idol," Henry mouthed, not knowing if he was speaking the name or thinking it or why he even knew it to begin with. Henry looked down at the hand in his grasp.

Alex crushed his fingers in a vice grip.

Alex twisted Henry forward and lurched to snag a caustic-looking Shirley Temple from the nearest table. He was in an eccentric blue business suit, smoking. His shoes were bright pink. Henry thought he looked like an arse.

But apparently, he was the arse, with the way Al was looking at him. It had to be about a girl, this he felt in his very bones. Henry's face turned ten shades of green. He reached for a drink from the table Alex had swiped his from; a shot of plain vodka.

"The fuck did you do?!" Alex gestured violently, speaking with his hands. From a maw-clenched cigarette, smoke spilled in ribbons to the ceiling above—a ceiling of damask and shadow. Henry blinked, and Tyr's painting flickered for a moment on that ceiling before being wiped away.

"S-sorry?" The brit coughed up his drink onto his blue shirt, "Ah, fack..." Henry sputtered, expressive eyes locked onto the color far too long for his pissed-off friend.

"*Eric*," Al's voice was a primal snarl. He leaned near 'Eric' and grabbed him by the shirt to drag his head down lower. With Al's face near his neck, he hissed like a viper into his ear.

"You need to tell her. **Now**."

"Mate, I can't do that...it'll break her tiny lil' candy heart, I canni—"

"You tell her. Or I will. And by tell her I mean beat the ever-loving shit—" Alex's voice raised in anger with every single word,"...shit out of you. In front of her," yet his sentence ended less violently, aware of where they were, and just how loud he was.

"Mate, I'm s—"

"What? You wanna' apologize?! Fucking apologize to Olive, you dim Brit fucknugget!" Alex spat, jerking 'Eric' forward by his shirt.

"Mate. I didn't make th' first move. An' I was drunk off me ass, spinnin' somethin' sideways, I dunno..."

Understanding flashed over Alex's features. In the low

light, the thrumming, bumping music, and the flickers of color, he was a feral beast.

"....Percy is dead," he seethed out a promise primed on hellfire and too-sweet alcohol.

"Y'don' get it mate..."

"When. When was it," spoke the blond in absolutes. Henry...Eric swallowed hard and removed Al's hands from his shirt, which was a difficult task as he'd apparently embedded his fingers into the cloth itself.

"Mate."

Al said nothing and stood back, his arms crossed, weight hefted on one leg, fuming. Alex wanted nothing more than to punch Eric until his face cracked like an egg and his brain matter spilled out all over the floor. Eric knew it.

"It was a week back, you was bein' my wingman—always proper at it—but this time, you was shit-faced an'..."

"No. No, fuck no. I didn't..." Alex's anger broke as realization struck him stupid. He pressed his flat palm into his face and groaned.

"We all 'ad a bit too much ta drink, but she was prolly fine. Or mostly fine. More fine than I was, mostly more fine. Prolly. An—"

"I pushed you to it...are you fucking *kidding* me!?"

"Naw, mate. I mean, yeh. Yeh you did bu', you know... we was both tossed."

Al took his sweet drink off the table and knocked it down his throat. Eric made a face. It must've tasted like some kind of dastardly cherry medicine. Why he enjoyed it was beyond him.

"...continue," Alex said, gesturing with his cigarette.

"She said, wha'ds she say...c'mon Eric, think...God damn— " Alex stared at him, not amused.

"She said, 'I want to do what I want. I don't want rules.' Somethin', somethin' bout you an' Liv foolin around, blah, complainin', then, breasts."

"...breasts?" Alex snorted.

"It was like she was made of 'em. Thas' all I 'member mate, swear. Scout's honor." Eric held up his pinky finger. Alex narrowed his eyes, took a sharp inhale of his cigarette, and scanned Eric's face.

"Scout's honor?" Alex looked Eric over, trying to find a hole in his story. Instead, he finagled his cigarette into an ashtray and raised his pinky.

"Scout's honor." They linked pinkies. The spat was over. Alex now had to redirect his rage elsewhere, which meant consuming more disgustingly sweet liquor.

Al glared behind his glass and looked over as Olive and Percy talked in a booth. They flirted, Olive shouted loudly, laughed, and Percy made a motion with her hands.

"Fix it," Al said as he sipped, the straw suctioning the ice in his glass.

"W...what?"

"Fix it, Erica. Fix it, fix it, fix it! Or so help me—"

"...I canni' go back in time, mate. Jus'," Eric raised his hands, hoping to field the assault he was going to get. Verbally or physically, a mad Alex was an Alex no one wanted to deal with.

It wasn't a good look getting yelled at for a straight hour or punched in the throat. Not that he had ever laid a hand on Eric. But for Olivia, he just might have.

"Go over there, now! Talk to them. Bring them outside. I don't care what you have to do, but make it right by her. She doesn't fucking deserve this."

Eric nodded, took a shot off of the table, and tipped his

head back. It burned down his throat as Al's eyes burned into his meaty skull.

He took a few steps. He saw wheat and grass again as he walked, but the bar remained the same. A part of a leafy green bush was in someone's drink. Purple flowers were in a woman's long red hair. He remembered this. He remembered living this. He remembered.

However, what he didn't remember was this scene from anyone else's point of view. It shifted. He was on the outside looking in as if pivoting on a 3D rig.

Alex watched the exchange as Eric took the girls outside. Percy looked at Alex, who was glaring daggers at her. Eric took Percy by the arm. She turned her head to lock eyes with the other blond. Terror swept over her guilty, guilty face.

Alex waved at her and blew her a kiss of death.

The trio went outside, and Alex stood by the doorway with his too-sweet drink, now refilled. Moira sauntered over to him with her hand on her hip and leaned. Intent on apparently showing herself off, Alex had to cast his eyes away from her chest.

"You want something, don't you?" Alex said, baby-blues looking anywhere but the femme fatale posturing in front of him.

"Trouble in paradise, darling?" Moira asked coyly.

"Yes." Alex raised a brow and leaned to look out the window. Percy was biting her lip and shifting in the cold. Alex couldn't see Eric's face. Olive was staring at the ground, eyes wide and face as pink as her hair.

"That's just horrible. Say, why don't you and I dance for a while? You can keep me company tonight. They'll obviously be indisposed." Moira stretched out her hand and played over his shoulder with delicate fingers.

"Nope."

"...nope? Nope? Why *nope*?" Moira pouted and twirled beside him. She was mildly intoxicated; he could tell because she was dancing. She never danced, and when she did, it was because she was up to no good.

"I'm not interested." Alex sipped his drink and didn't meet her predatory gaze.

"Why not, dear? Don't tell me you've switched teams completely—"

"Nope, I play for whatever team I want. It's because I don't...trust a lot of people right now."

Moira looked hurt but played it off by sauntering closer and threading her hands over his shoulders to clasp around the back of his neck.

"You don't trust me, pet? I-I'm not like that *terrible* European," Moira protested, "He'd been so awful to you...and have I not been very, very good?" Moira tilted her head, pretty as a posey, and gave him a beautiful smile.

"Of course you have. It's just..." Moira pouted as Alex spoke, leaning her head to his chest. Alex looked down at her and closed his eyes, "I'm fragile right now, and you suck at fragile."

"You don't have to be mean about it, dear..." Moira mumbled into Alex's blue suit. His expression softened. Alex kissed the top of her head.

"...you're not my type..." he whispered into her hair, more gentle than he had been before.

"Your type comes in a far taller package, with a package, doesn't it?" she teased, wrapping her around his shoulders, "and calls you crazy, in so many words. I don't know why you date men who hurt you so—"

"Nope. Not always."

Alex looked through the window and saw Olivia burst into tears. He could hear their entire conversation. Moreover, he could hear Olive crying through the window. Her sobs were brutal. Deep, painful wails bolted from her body. In between words, underneath them, and through them. A devastated pixie.

"Ya think I'd ever do that c-crap? He's a friend, and yer—you're a-a bitch!" Olive screeched, tears rolling down her face, "Percy, you've r-ruined everything!"

"I just thought, like...you know..." Percy began but stopped. Olive was shaking. The blonde woman took her into her arms. Olive sobbed into Percy's chest, seeking comfort even in the arms of the person who had hurt her most.

"You misjudge her, mate. An' it's on me too, it is," Henry heard himself say. The rig shifted; Olive was in front of him now.

He stretched out a hand to her, but the sun went out again as if clasped in a constricting fist.

He turned over his palm in the air, and he felt warmth in his grasp. He felt movement, a weight between his fingers. A palm in his hand that extended to an arm. An arm that extended to a woman, a woman who had broken the heart of someone very undeserving of it.

The wheat fields came back. He was walking behind Polly. She looked over her shoulder.

"...are you listening to me? God, whatever..." Polly scoffed.

"Sorry, Polly. I was...remembrin'...somethin'...like when yeh told me 'boutcha' dream, an' all," Henry said, still tethered to her fingers.

"Oh? Oh....Oh!" Polly said, turning to walk backward so

she could look at Henry as they spoke, "Like...what happened?" she blurted out, her face bathed in gold from the sun.

She snatched his hand yet again.

"We were roight shit to 'er. Pepto. Roight shit," Henry said with a sour expression.

"Pepto?" Polly paused, "...we were?" Polly frowned.

"Yeh. Shit. But...I think it turnt out awright...s'awright as it coulda." Henry looked crestfallen. Then, his dark brown eyes sparked with muddy thoughts of the time before—scanning, searching, thinking, which was, as always, not his strong suit.

"Like...why do you say that?" she asked.

"Cuz I think somethin' else happened later. Somethin' brilliant," Henry replied, shaking his head, "I dunno. S'foggy, like I'm missin' stuff."

Henry took Polly by the arm as they walked, elbows linked, and emerged from the field. It was then that Polly finally saw the message from Virginia. The one she'd sent that no one else—save Vox—had received.

'Maya. Taken. Library. Diana. Not Responding. Help. Please.'

Her deep brown eyes opened wide.

"Henry," Polly said, trying to get the man's attention, "Henry, something happened. We, like, have to go right now..."

Henry wasn't looking at her. He was looking in the distance at the fields of gold. The fields of gold that were now smoldering with searing hellfire.

A GIANT MECHANIZED creature barreled through The Greens. It tore through the dirt and the trees, ripped up the landscape, and flooded the field with broken rocks and earth. It was massive and far faster than anything either of them had seen in any lifetime.

"Oh...oh my G—" Henry grabbed Polly's hand, halted her sentence, and tore her through the tall grass, jerking her behind him. Faster than her legs could carry her. Faster than his could carry him.

The machine was silver with spots of plastic, shining like an oil slick, and behind it came an ocean of guards in black. Too many guards. The pair had no weapons; this was happening too quickly.

"Fack me—" Henry cursed as he barreled over a mound of wheat and jerked Polly over it, who struggled but cut through it nonetheless.

"We have to hide! Where?!" Polly smashed her damp, naked leg past a ragged rock and let out a short yelp. Polly was dragged through the fields with Henry as her lifeline, like a puppet on a mach-powered string, leaving behind a trail of poppy blood.

"I got a place. I got a place. We jus' gotta make it to the water."

"W-what?" Polly screeched.

"MOVE," Henry screamed, jerking her through a wall of wheat.

Polly ran with him. The grass now cut her feet, and the stones dug into raw, shredded flesh. Henry yanked her faster, hard enough to bruise her wrist, and finally just hefted her over his shoulder and ran as fast as he could.

Henry ran, charting through The Greens as people screamed and fled, dispersing like dye in the waters of singed gold and burning earth.

A laser scalped through the earth behind them; a cyan incision.

"We get in; we dive," Henry shouted. A huge crash of a laser skewered a nearby tree as it sought the pair of humans, focusing the beam like a searching eye. The tree exploded into flames.

"Aaaah!" Polly shrieked, but it was Henry who gripped her harder. He jumped over a bush and held onto Polly's rear as she bounced over his shoulder, staring at the giant machination fast approaching. Its laser stopped for a few spare moments, then it reoriented and raged towards them in a long line of cyan.

"It's getting closer, Henry! Henry! Go faster!" Polly screeched, pounding at his back with her fists.

"Woman, I'm goin' as fast as I can. Shut it fer once in ya bloody life!" he bellowed out as Polly screwed her mouth shut.

They made it to the water, and Henry flung Polly into it.

Polly dove immediately. He followed after, hoping she could hold her breath long enough to make it.

Cool water closed in around them. Polly scraped at it with her fingers, faltering. The current at the bottom of the river was far faster than it had been near the surface. Yet Polly found her footing and surged ahead, kicking her long limbs; fight or flight, do or die, the time is now. Henry lagged behind.

Polly reeled back, snatched him by the hair with her nails, and dragged him towards a dark spot. A cave. She saw a cave. Henry struggled, but Polly pulled him forward. The two kicked and cut through the current. There was a cave; it was in reach, just one more kick.

They surfaced, both gasping for breath.

BACK ON THE JUDICIAL LEVEL, Maya was still yet held captive. Breathing heavy into the black bag around her head, she fought back bitter tears. She was being moved. She could hear the clink of metal on the floor.

She could hear guttural screams. The guards were growing more aggressive with her. Dragging her around by her cuffs like a heavy sack, they swapped her at some point.

She heard a laser rifle go off. She heard doors being slammed, cussing, and heavy footsteps. Then she heard what sounded like someone drowning.

Maya was let go with a jerk. Something fell with a dull thud next to her. She heard footsteps—someone running. Then she heard her heart beating fast, the blood rushing in her ears. Light footsteps came forward, heavier on one leg; a saunter.

The bag came up over her head, and all she saw were blindingly blue eyes.

Maya stared into Alex's eyes, tears streaming down her face. As ragged breaths shuttered her body, she screwed her eyes shut. He was speaking to her, but she couldn't hear him. All she heard was her heartbeat.

When she opened her eyes, she realized she was being held not by the blond synth war machine but by a woman who looked curiously like Polly.

Maya sobbed as the blond woman held her close. It was dark; she was outside. The building near them had flashing lights inside; they were too bright. A guilty-looking man was there. He was tall as an oak tree, with strong brows and broad shoulders.

Their faces were ones she knew. She knew this place. She knew this woman. She knew she'd loved this woman. She knew.

"Percy, you've r-ruined everything!" she felt herself scream out in a shattered voice. Percy held her as she cried hot, wet tears. If Percy or Eric were speaking, Maya was no longer listening. She couldn't. She could do nothing but cry.

The sound of an engine cut her wailing. A motorcycle drew up beside her. She tried to see it through the blur of her tears.

Alex walked over and grabbed her by the back of the shirt. He had his helmet on, but the visor was up.

"Let's go," Alex said. He pulled her towards his body. She didn't resist, red-eyed and disoriented.

"Mate...Please don't kill me," Eric said, completely serious.

"You're fine. You're stupid but not an asshole," Alex spat, wielding the small woman in his grasp, "But you, Percy. Don't do anything like this ever again. Or you're—" Alex stopped his threat and grumbled, "I'll...stop paying for your shit. All of it. No more living off my dime. You hear me?"

Percy looked at him and then looked at the cobbled

ground. She wouldn't apologize. She shot Alex the most visceral glare she had. Alex ignored her.

"Olive, wanna' get out of here?" Al stooped to ask 'Olive', who nodded her head vigorously into his side.

Alex pried the extremely reluctant Olive off of him and sat her on the motorcycle. Turning, he got out his spare helmet from the side-bag and placed it on her head. She made a slight noise of discomfort. He pushed down on the helmet and chuckled.

He swung his leg over the machine, kicked out the stand, started the motorcycle up, and they were off.

It was loud. The wind rushed. Olive was getting cold. She was exhausted. She didn't want to be here. Her heart hurt. Everything inside of her was breaking apart.

"Open your eyes, princess," his muffled words made it to her ears despite the air whipping around them, "C'mon. Open your eyes," Alex repeated, louder this time.

Olivia did, and she saw the lights of the city rush by as they made it towards the bay. The lights reflected off the water and shone in a stream like a million LEDs. They were going impossibly fast.

Purple clouds smeared across the skyline as they busted through a side-alley and took a sharp turn to whisk up to a bright, delicious-smelling borough.

People were still chatting this late at night, drinking warm drinks, singing, laughing. The neon signs were loud enough to compete with the stars above. All of it was a stream of color, scent, sound, and light. All of it was beautiful, if blinding.

Then, the engine died, and Olive looked around at where they were, blurry-eyed and shaken. They were in Chinatown, but which one, she couldn't say.

Alex helped her off of the motorcycle.

With her small hand in his own, he walked with her. The two of them were still wearing their helmets. They passed the cramped restaurant that made its home beneath his flat. At the door, Alex looked down at the short woman but said nothing. He was thinking.

Olive's apartment was lined with memories of Percy. It was an in-law apartment off of her parents' house. She had comic books, collectible cards, and figurines. Even though she had been a messy kid, she learned to clean up and be self-sufficient as an adult—more so when she had started dating Percy.

Going back there now would have done nothing but crush her. Her comics and posters wouldn't make it any better. Alex knew it, and so, here they were.

Alex hesitated at the door of his apartment.

"Do you want some dumplings?" he asked. Olive nodded her response, the large helmet bobbing over her messy pink curls.

"Pork?" Olive nodded at his question.

Alex stalked to the small dumpling shop that made up the real estate below his flat. He knocked on the dingy window.

"Four pork buns with dipping sauce, please. Thanks, Yu." The man behind the window pulled it open and glared at Alex, then tossed a glance at the girl idling on his steps.

"Never seen this short girl come by...is it because you're messy? Hiding your pig-sty from the pink one? I've only seen you take out the trash once! Once!" crooned the man.

"Shut up, Yuen," Alex joked and slid Yuen a fifty-dollar bill across the silver counter.

"Hey, hey, hey. You can't bribe me!" Yuen yelled through the window.

"Bribe you? What am I bribing you for?" Al placed his hand on his hip and quirked a brow from underneath his helmet.

"Your 'illegal activities,'" Yuen said bluntly.

"Like what, Yuen? Being too loud? Feeding stray cats?" Alex snorted through the helmet.

"Yes! It's the cats!" the man roared, "They're loud and mess up my dumpsters!" Yuen wagged his finger at Alex, who just laughed him off with a hearty chuckle.

"Alright, alright, old man."

"And they piss everywhere!" Yuen barked but inevitably ceased his tirade because it was clear Alex wasn't listening to him.

Their food was soon made, wrapped with wax paper with love and care. Yuen had placed them in a small box, pulled the crinkling paper over them, and taped the paper before closing the lid. The box was patterned in bright red flowers. Yuen sealed it with a small daisy sticker.

"For you. All set. Thank you."

"Thanks, Yuen. You're the best," Alex replied, taking the boxed food in hand.

"Yes! That's right! I am!" he chortled, "Don't forget it!"

"Yeah, yeah, yeah," Alex shouted back at Yuen as he rounded to where Olive was standing.

"Mmph," Olive tried to speak through the helmet that was far too large for her.

Alex hefted the box under his arm and held out his hand to guide Olive up the steps. She took his grasp and followed, her head bobbing as she ascended.

They entered the flat. It was covered in clothes and pizza

boxes. Vinyl records were stacked in one corner, and there were cups with mold in them on various shelves. Yuen had been right; clearly, Alex had only taken out the trash all of one time during his entire stay in the once-lovely, now-disgusting flat.

"How can ya live in this?" Olive finally spoke, her voice muffled by the helmet.

"Hmm?" Alex kicked a pizza box off the sofa and sat down with his feet up. He took off his helmet.

Olivia unbuckled her helmet and jerked it over her head, her hair flattened. She dropped it to the floor with a muffled thunk. With a vicious shake, the curls sprung free, albeit freer than they needed to. She looked like a pink shrub. Alex didn't comment on it.

"I said how can ya live like this?! It's gross!" the little thing spat, gawking at the disarray that was his bachelor pad, "Is this how tha' rest of it is? Oh, yuck…"

"I haven't been home in a while. I've been…working. I've had Yuen feed Diana though," he replied, oblivious to the mess.

"Diana?" Olivia squinted through her blurry eyes. She caught the records at the far end of the room flickering from her peripheral vision. They stopped stuttering when he spoke again.

"My cat," he said with a quirked half-smile.

"You have a cat?" Olivia asked, brows turned up.

"Moira, Diana, Diana, Moira…why is she named after tha' cat?" Olive asked, scanning his face for an answer he couldn't quite give her.

"Yes, I have a cat. And, what the shit does *that* mean?"

Olive looked at Alex, who was sitting with his helmet in his lap, his bright eyes giving her nothing but gentleness.

"This is crazzyyy...can I change this?" she asked herself, squinting at the disaster zone that was Alex's apartment.

"What?" he asked, brows twisting up as he leaned over his helmet.

"...the past?" Olive trailed her question as if testing the words in her mouth. Alex snorted at her half-question.

"Did you have anything to drink?" Alex asked with a dry smile as he pulled out his pack of cigarettes and smacked the bottom of the carton to his palm.

Olive wandered over and sat beside him, dropping into the sofa as if it'd suck her into a portal and pop her out into the present. She might have even tried to wriggle down into it to achieve just that.

"Al, yer gonna be very strong and very weak later. But I need ya' to know, after all this, that I am going to protect you. Okay?"

"Liv, what the fuck are you talking about?" he asked, hitting the carton to his palm again.

"...just remember, okay? Ya aren't alone."

With that, the blond raised a brow and lit up a cigarette. He placed the carton on the table and went back to glancing over at his short friend.

"I know I'm not. Do you...know you aren't either?"

Olive looked over Alex's face. She looked to the mess, to the cigarette, to the helmet in his lap, and said nothing.

Olive rested her head on his arm. Moments passed, and she rolled her face to his shoulder. Alex shifted her to wrap his arm around her shoulder and pull her to his chest. He tapped his cigarette ash directly onto the floor, which made her grimace. They sat like this for a time; Alex smoked, she nestled, they breathed, and simply existed.

"...yeah," she mumbled through a sleepy mouth, eyes red and brows knit.

"Yeah?" Alex asked, looking down at the mass of pink curls nestled to his arm.

"Mhm..."

"Are you getting tired?" he asked.

"Mhm..."

"Wanna go to sleep?"

"Mhm..."

Alex moved Olive aside and picked her up in his arms, his cigarette clenched between his teeth. He placed her on his bed, which was the only thing that wasn't totally covered in junk, and pulled her coat off. He tossed the Barney monstrosity aside. It smelled like coffee.

As he pulled a blanket over her, the cat jumped into the bed to join her. She mewled and rolled onto her back to shadow-box with the blankets, but Olivia didn't stir.

Olive's eyes closed.

"You look like a mess," he said under his breath, then sheepishly looked around his room, his hand over his mouth.

"But not as big of a mess as...ah fuck...I gotta clean this shit up..." he said, his voice was a whisper. Alex looked back at his friend, and his expression softened.

"Percy's such an ass..."

Olivia had a particular reverence for the valley-girl Percival; one Alex had never truly understood. Sure, he loved her, but she was prone to ruining any good thing she had out of spite. However, he had seen that reverence in action once when hunting for liquor. They'd crashed at Eric's place after a brutal party.

Olive had pattered about in her raglan shirt and colorful

sweats, sidling next to Percy, who was sleeping on a bunch of blankets in Eric's living room. Gentle fingers had moved over a bit of blonde hair to see Percy's face better. She had leaned in for a brief kiss and then rolled away to smile to herself.

Alex had smiled too, then went on the hunt to rifle through Eric's cabinets and fridge.

But now, there was no smile on Olive's face. As she slept, she looked anything but happy. At times her eyes screwed shut in pain and then flicked open for just a moment as she rolled over.

Alex didn't sleep in his bed that night. He hadn't slept in his own bed in weeks anyway, and now, he'd have to get used to that again. After all, he'd all but moved into Markov's place.

However, Alex did lay next to Olive for a moment with his head resting on his hand. He did move a bit of her pink hair out of her face as she snored. He did place a small kiss on her forehead.

Before he left to crash on his sofa, he did let a smile sweep across his face. He'd mimicked the ritual she'd reserved for Percy.

A makeshift panacea; it's all he felt he could do. He would've killed to see her happy if given the chance.

Maya knew this now and didn't know why she did—why she felt how he felt in that moment—why she'd been awake to see it. She didn't know why she could even see, feel, taste, touch, and experience all of this to begin with.

None of this made any sense to her.

Time didn't fall away as it had for Henry. For Maya, she simply opened her eyes from sleep, and there Alex was. There he was, as he had been before, focusing only on her.

"Let's get out of here," he said.

"Give me a gun," she replied, no longer shaken but her gaze distant. Alex didn't hesitate and gave her the actual gun, the one with bullets.

"It has a—my name—on it..." Scratched out in tiny letters was the name 'Olive'. *Olivia. Liv. Livvie.*

Maya cocked the weapon and ran out towards the hallway, with Al trailing behind her. Then, she stepped in something. She stopped and smelled the air, iron and rust hitting her like a freight train.

Maya looked down at the floor at the dead guard who had jerked away from her earlier, blood pooling out of his body. Her gaze trailed to linger on Alex, the gun held loosely in her grasp. Her shoulders scrunched instinctually.

Alex stepped over the body, with Maya still standing in the red lake. She picked up her foot and stepped onto the white floor. A pattern of shoe prints trailed after her.

She saw why he wasn't in a rush to hand her the gun to defend herself. She saw why he didn't seem fearful they'd be caught.

"Ya killed...everybody," Maya whispered.

Secretaries, municipal workers, random people. The only ones left were synths, who gave him knowing nods and began to clean up.

This, he had let Tyr see. In fact, he was seeing it right now.

Tyr was sitting in his marble throne room, staring at a holographic display projected from a place unseen. His face was destroyed, but lucky for him, he lived in a time where these things were easily remedied.

A medical bot hummed at his ear and spread a grid of light over his skin. It was doing its job perfectly, just as it was programmed to; it could treat humans, synths, and slight structural damage—a perfect tool with many uses.

When Tyr leaned over his table, the medical bot followed his movement. He was staring straight at the events that had just unfolded, the ones Alex had wanted him to see, judging by how gratuitous it all was.

Blood coated the walls in a masterwork of viscera. Tyr rewound the display with a press to a curious indent in his palm. He froze the recording on a frame that showed Alex striking a man through the chest with his bare fist. Alex's fingers had grasped actual guts, and he had smiled.

In this video feed, Alex clutched the meat between his digits and tore. A fountain of tangled flesh came forth through cracked ribs. The blond war machine unearthed an organ; a heart. He shoved the heart into the man's mouth, past his teeth, and down his throat.

This was Alex's response to Tyr's actions; a play in blood, a direct response, a show of his power.

Tyr pressed the indent on his palm again, and the scene flipped through until he rested on a particular frame. Tyr pressed, and the image zoomed in to land on Alex's face.

Alex stared straight at the camera and smiled. Then he bit into his lower lip, vicious and loving every moment of it.

"You...petulant, filthy maggot..." hissed Tyr. Tyr's careful control had been obliterated in one smile from a demon of metal.

Tyr heard a short, dry laugh from beyond one of his fountains.

"Stop playing games, Sebastian. I know you're here," Tyr spat through clenched teeth. The medical bot whirred and jittered, following Tyr around as he moved. He glared daggers into the small machine; it trilled a beep in response.

"Uncle," said the voice.

"Nephew," Tyr parroted back, narrowing his eyes to thin slits.

Sebastian hesitated but finally strode from the shadows to rest beside one of Tyr's golden fountains.

Tyr's nephew was an Appolyon youth with large eyes and dark hair. His brows were fair enough that his expression was often unreadable. His general attire was subtle as well but hardly inexpressive. Every article of clothing told a story, from the mature brown business casual-attire to the smart leather shoes.

"He beat you. Not surprising." Sebastian said with a confidence beyond his years.

"Not another word, Sebastian."

"...is that what you're pissed about?" Sebastian saun-tered towards Tyr and gave him a smirk.

"I told you he would." The medical bot chirped as if in response.

"Shut your mouth, welp," Tyr seethed, sitting back to jab at his palm again and cycle through more images. Sebastian kept speaking, much to Tyr's absolute disdain.

"You didn't listen," Sebastian said, "I've seen him kill a man with a toothpick and win a fight using a fork."

"And how could you possibly—"

The youth stood poker-straight, squaring his shoulders to appear intimidating. His uncle was a behemoth in comparison. To be plain, he was a behemoth to everyone else as well.

"I told you that the minute you let your guard down, he'd kill you." The medical bot beeped as Sebastian spoke.

"I told you he was different. I told you he'd fight you each step of the way, even if it seemed he'd given in. I told you all of this, and you didn't believe me."

Tyr wheeled around with the force of a typhoon, struck towards Sebastian, grabbed his face with his fingers and squeezed his cheeks to the point of bruising.

"Youths should be seen and not heard. Where is your mother?!"

Sebastian pulled away and held his jaw, rubbing at the tender skin Tyr had accosted.

"Ow...busy, I guess. I'm unsure."

"Why are you here?!" Tyr spat, glaring down at the young man who tilted his head to the side, scanning his uncle's slowly reconstructing face.

"I was hoping you'd get offed, and I'd be able to sit in your shiny transparent chair and make the puppets dance."

Tyr shot Sebastian a glare, studying his inexpressive face for a scrap of an answer; from where did this petulance live?

"...and how would you make them dance?" Tyr asked, momentarily fascinated.

"Democratically," Sebastian said simply. He folded his arms across his chest and leaned against the fountain's ledge,"...do you want help?" Sebastian asked, expression still unreadable.

"...yes," Tyr responded, the word a weakness in his mouth.

"Good," Sebastian replied with a dull smile, "...because I'm not going to give it to you."

"Unless you give me everything I want, of course."

ON THE JUDICIAL LEVEL, Diana had watched the events of Alex's massacre unfold from a janitor's closet. She had opened the door a little, being careful not to leave herself exposed. Her eyes strained to see the bloodshed through the small crack.

A flickering light passed over and through the door. It painted a thin line over her honey-colored skin. Like a smear of yellow ochre and titanium white, the light bled out into the shadow of her face. She hid. The light flickered. She looked.

Bodies dropped like falling stars.

She could see the pools made of iron, colored in rust. She could see shadows as they passed over the door and through that painted line of light.

There were screams. A stray bullet blew past her head and busted open a bottle of cleaner. Diana hadn't screamed.

The sound of gunfire and laser blasts drew her attention. They sounded far away. Then close again. Then far once more. Finally, she heard the carnage right in front of her.

She cracked the door open with her foot. Her cheek was

bathed in bright blue. Diana slunk back into the closet. The light blinded her, then faded. Another blast, and another fade.

During the events that transpired in the library, she hadn't helped Maya escape. If Diana was dethroned, she knew where they'd put her and what it would mean for their delicate, if vague, operation.

Maybe she'd be placed as a beautiful gyrating ornament in The Blue Room on Tyr's level; she'd heard stories. Maybe worse than that by leaps and bounds—the unimaginable Reds, which she now imagined.

The Reds were entire levels dedicated to sin. They had red lights, red signs, and white letters. They had hot white fear, and blood red bodies.

The Reds were nothing like The Blue Room.

Another shot resounded beside her head. Diana ducked instinctively.

A smell caught her nose—cleaning solutions—she accidentally kicked a bottle with her heel. It made a swishing noise and then fell over, toppling a few others, spreading cleaner on the floor from the bullet hole.

Maya's head turned to look her way. Diana's heart started to bleat like a stuck lamb.

Then the little squirrel turned her attention back to Alex, and they were off.

Diana admitted to herself that at this moment, she was scared. Not scared of the gunfire or the bodies. Not scared of the Reds, the Blue Room, the blood, the death, of being poor, used, and mistreated.

"He's a monster," she whispered to herself.

Diana peered on as the two seemed far away. She knelt and tried to scrape the soap off of her heel with her hand.

Diana heard a noise; rushing water. She pulled her long hair behind her ear and crouched low. Scanning for sound, and yet she couldn't figure out where it was coming from.

Wheeling around, Diana slipped in suds and fell back onto her rear with a muted shriek.

The lights flickered inside of the closet. Diana looked down at her feet as she struggled to stand. Her heels were gone. She was wearing sneakers. She felt hot and sticky, although the atmospheric control was fine on this level. The rushing, rushing water...

It was all too much.

"Enough!"

When she raised herself up off her rear, she was stooping over a sink with gloves on her hands. Her long hair was pinned underneath a fishnet cap. She had a plate in her grasp. Diana narrowed her eyes, raised her brows, and let her mouth hang open.

A door at the far end opened, startling her. A man kept it open with his back. He was talking to someone she couldn't see. Beyond him, men were laughing loudly. A table was slammed with what she assumed was a fist. The man speaking near the door distracted her.

Water was running over the brim of the sink.

"Moira! Earth to Moira..." A large, gaunt man with tired eyes approached her.

"Um...lo siento...er.." Moira shook her head and turned the water off. He stood next to her and folded his arms across his chest. The adjacent door opened wider. She grew distracted again as she caught a flash of a tacky shirt. The door swung back again.

"Every extra minute you leave the water on, we have to pay for it...Moi, this is the fourth time..." She heard the sound of gunfire. The man talking to her didn't flinch as she had. He hadn't heard it.

"But it was only for a sec! Hey, hey…I'm sorry. I…" Moira put the plate in the sink, which caused more water to flow over the rim. She reached out to the man.

Bright green gloves left suds on his shirt. He pulled back, but she kept her hold on him. The door creaked shut, then opened just a crack, held open by a hand.

"Please, please…I gotta make rent this month…" she pleaded, "Please!"

"Alright, Moira. But this is the last time. One more strike, and you're out, got it?"

"I got it. I got it…"

She didn't remember finishing up the rest of her shift but she must have because she was sitting at a bar when she came out of her stress-induced stupor.

She smelled like soap, and her hair was still matted under the fishnet cap. With pruned fingers, worn and red, she pulled the cap off and shook her tresses free. Her beautiful, dark curls didn't fall in waves of ocean.

She pulled out tangled knots.

Moira sat at the bar and asked for the cheapest drink they had. She caught the reflection of herself in a silver bottle behind the bartender, and she felt her heart skip a beat.

"Don't like the drink?"

"No, no, it's not that…" Moira held a mug of warm beer in her hand and sipped on it. Resting her head on her hand, elbow to the table, she stared at the ruddy, somewhat glossy surface. She stared at herself and didn't recognize the woman who stared back.

The door clattered open without concern for the other patrons—which were few and far between. Men in nice outfits with thick accents came through in a pack. The one at the front was very tall. The one beside him was short for a guy.

They were hollering and gesturing, the two at the front seemingly far calmer than the other three ruffians. The trio intended to make as much of a ruckus as possible—arms out into the air as they talked with their hands.

Laughter. Groaning. Excitement. Almost screaming in that low, bellowing way that excited men scream. Like at sporting events. She hated sports.

"Damn loud-ass motherfuckers..." Moira spat, not so quietly, and twisted her face into a grimace.

The dishwasher sipped on her beer and watched the men as they sat at a large booth. All of them sat like they were trying to air out their family jewels.

Save one: the shorter one, who had his elbow on the table like her own—resting his head. His gaze traveled across the room until it landed on her face.

He had a certain type of smile; if looks could kill and beckon all at once, that was what his mouth was doing. As his brows raised, her brows fell. Moira looked away and guzzled down more beer. She knew what was going to happen next.

The taller man slapped a hand to the shorter one's back and then gestured at Moira with his other hand. They exchanged words she couldn't hear. The shorter man held up his hands sheepishly. The taller man let his hand stay at the shorter one's shoulder.

She saw the taller man lean ever so slightly closer to the shorter man's face.

"Fucking Maloso..." she seethed into her beer mug and took another deep swig.

The taller man gave a slight glance to the shorter one and moved his arm away. He folded his hands on the table and leaned forward. He tilted his head slightly. The two spoke, and the shorter man played with a napkin, peeling at the paper.

Moira didn't miss the look as the shorter man suffered to hide a smile, went quiet, and looked off towards the entrance; a wistful expression.

The dishwasher cocked an eye and knocked back more of her beer. She felt a burp coming, so she pounded her fist into her chest and let it announce itself.

It was louder than she'd expected. The entire table had heard her. The men were staring.

"Um...sorry..." she said, not really sorry at all. She stifled a yawn as best she could. It had been an incredibly long day for her.

The shorter guy stood up. The taller one shifted in his seat, no longer leaning forward. He let his hands rest in his lap. The taller man had taken notice of her again.

Had he not expected him to come over to her? The tall man looked on as the shorter man—blond and plucky—walked over to Moira. The taller one resumed his conversations with the others.

Someone slammed their fist onto the table, and there were cheers as a waitress brought them their drinks.

"Vodka? What are you, walking stereotypes?" Moira grumbled into her beer.

The would-be femme fatale chugged down the rest of her beer, wiped her mouth on her sleeve, and grabbed her bag. She was going to make her escape. These men were making her uncomfortable as most men did, late at night, in bars.

But none of them made her more uncomfortable than the

oddly dressed blond fellow with a gun tucked into the back of his pants. There was no doubt this dive bar was one of 'their' hangouts.

Or maybe even a front.

"The one day I decide to try a new bar...ugh..." she said, still not aware of her volume level.

The shorter 'Maloso' hopped up on the stool next to her. She froze. He was wearing an obnoxious tourist shirt with sewn-on patches all over it. His jeans were black and torn up. He wasn't well dressed like the others.

One particular patch caught her attention. Thick bold letters, the last letter was backward. It was familiar, but Moira was struggling to place it.

The blond sat with a slight slump to his shoulders and looked at her. He was resting his head on his palm, elbow to the table, as she had done earlier. He shot her a cheeky smile.

"You know, you're awfully clever to be working as a dishwasher. Or was it a waitress? Or was it a singer? A model, actress?"

"E-excuse me? Um..." Moira shirked away as he spoke.

"You've got a hairnet stuffed in your purse. I tried to flag you down earlier. Plus, we've already—"

"Ah...um...yeah, yeah...well...clever don't mean shit..."

"Sure it does," he said with a cheshire smile.

The blond ordered the same beer she was having and played his fingers around the rim of the mug for a few moments. He looked into the glass and quirked a smile before taking a sip.

"See, a girl like you could get whatever she wanted. If she was clever. You really don't rememb—"

"You...really think so?" Moira cut him off abruptly.

"I know so. You think I got to where I am with just

brute strength alone? Fuck no," he took another sip, "...there are a lot of ways to get ahead. Some more obvious than others."

Moira looked at his features with a squint. No, he had to be clever, even if he didn't look like it. Unless he knew how to kill a man with a fork or something.

"I mean, you already know what we do. It's obvious—you're pretty bright, which is why you were going to get the hell out of dodge before I sat next to you. And why your hand is desperately clutching your bag more tightly than I'd handle someone's throat," he said, ending on a quaint chuckle.

"You're...an arrogant little dog, aren't you?" she said with a sneer. He laughed.

"Yes, yes I am. But you already knew that, didn't you?"

Moira swept off of the stool and tried to shuffle away, but he just kept speaking.

"Wait, you seriously don't—" Moira jabbed her hand into her bag, pulled out her pepper-spray, pressed her finger down, and maced the blond man in the face.

"You...stupid idiot...I'm trying to—" The man grasped his eyes and groaned. His companions began to laugh hysterically.

"Give you a...fucking...opportunity...that we've already —" he gripped the hem of his shirt and rubbed it over his face, "Fuck! It burns!" he screeched through the tears that came.

The man fell to his knees. The taller man started to laugh, deep in his chest. It rose above all the other laughter in the room. The peanut gallery chimed in.

"Eh, брат...hairnet woman with bad taste in beer took you down. With bottle of girl spray."

"Aha! Girl spray. Like perfume!" piped up another buffoon with slick hair and a large nose.

"Who is big strong man now, eh?"

"It's mace you fucking inbred piece of—fuck," the short Maloso struggled.

Moira smirked and placed a hand over her mouth to giggle. She knelt in front of him and took him by the hand. He fought with her hand, but it was useless.

"You...really weren't trying to start something, were you?" She tried to pry his hands away from his face.

"No, I'm not that kind of guy. And we've already had this—not every guy is trying to get into your pants or sell you on the black fucking market, you know..." the blond grimaced.

"Let me see," she pawed at his face.

"No," he protested, jerking away.

"Let me see," she was more insistent this time, prying his fingers from his eyes, one by one.

"...fine."

Moira started to cackle.

"You poor, poor boy—"

The blond joined in her laughter, and the two started into fits. Moira was snorting, and the man was trying to laugh while also wincing and screwing his eyes shut. He stopped every few seconds to rub at them, which made matters worse.

The taller man at the table stood up and walked over to them. The sound of his smart leather shoes made Moira stop laughing, but the blond continued.

"Alex, you'll be fine. But flush out your eyes," the taller man paused, "As for you..." Moira skittered back over the floor, sneakers squeaking.

"Calm down. I'm not going to hurt you...don't mace me." Moira's hand gripped the pepper-spray as she stared up at this giant in a brown suit, "Please."

She held it up. The tall man raised up his hands and then knelt by Alex, dropping to his knees.

"Please, miss," he continued.

"What the fuck do I do!?" Alex spat, rubbing his eyes furiously.

"Wash your eyes out, like I said. Go to the sink," said the taller man.

"Fuck no, Boris is going to try to take her away in his child-abductor minivan..." Alex protested, yet again rubbing his eyes.

"She'll be fine. She'll be fine," the taller man reassured the blond.

Alex grunted and stood up, using the other man's shoulder as leverage. Then he half-walked, half-stumbled towards the bar. The bartender pointed to the bathroom. Alex waved him away and popped into the bathroom with a slam of the door.

"You're rather dangerous." The taller man spoke to her in deep, earthy tones. Slightly European, probably a bit less than the man who she had just maced right in the eyes. He was very clearly the leader of this group.

Moira was still on the ground with her weapon raised.

"S-so are you..." she spoke, low in the throw.

"Hmm. Well, yes...most locals know not to go here," he said plainly.

"I just stumbled in! I had a bad day! Alright!?" Moira spat, shoved her mace into her bag, then screwed it shut with a rip of the zipper.

She hefted herself to her knees and then stood, her bag clutched in a knuckle-white grip.

The tall man was still kneeling, but he met her gaze before coming up on his knee, hand to it, steadying himself to stand.

"¡Ay, Dios mío! You're tall," she marveled, craning her head to look up at the man.

"Yes. Yes, I am," the giant replied.

"Now, are you going to behave?" he spoke like a school teacher.

"....no," Moira blurted out, "Yes. I mean. No...I was just here for a beer."

"That's fine. But it's best you don't come here again. Especially alone."

The tall man lit up a cigarette and offered her one, she declined.

"...what's your name?"

"Moira," she said, still yet unsure.

"I'm Mark." The other man was overflowing with quiet, subdued confidence. He didn't need to put on airs about being powerful; he just was. But there was something else—something unreadable about his expression that unnerved her.

"...Russian?" she asked, squinting at Mark.

"Yes. You?"

"Hey, Markov...I think I got it all out," Alex interrupted the pair, having appeared behind them, rubbing his eyes, "the acoustics in this place are fucking awful. I could literally hear Boris scratching his balls from the stall—" Alex's ramblings were ignored.

"Puerto Rican," she said, gesturing with her chin to the blond man behind her, "....him?"

"Annoying, but...very useful," Markov said.

"...them?" Moira gestured at the peanut gallery.

"Idiots." Markov smoked and looked her over. His body was relaxed, but he held tension in his fists. Moira, contrary to that, was solidly full of nerves so tight she might've snapped like a rubber band.

Markov twisted around and looked over the blond man.

"Al, you look like you got high and fell down a flight of stairs..." Markov said, a curious grin spreading across his handsome face.

"Thanks, Mark—" the blond started.

"And like you got hit by a truck," the taller man continued, smoke ribboning the air around him.

"Thanks, Mark—"

"And like you fell out of an ugly tree and smacked every branch on the way dow—"

"Alright! Markov. Shut the fuck up already!" Alex spat but quickly changed focus. The blond rounded to Moira's side and attempted his sales pitch again, kneeling beside her on the balls of his feet.

"I'm surprised you don't even remember me," he was still blinking wildly, "we've already—"

"I'm not becoming one of those 'red light' girls, rollin' on their backs for money," she cut Alex off.

"I'm not asking that of you," Alex said, holding up his hands, "I never would. We're just going outside. You can mace me if I'm lying."

Alex looked to Markov with just one eye open. Markov glanced over the shorter man's face.

"Just what are you planning, little bird?" Markov asked, fascinated.

"Something awesome. God, how many times have I asked you to stop calling me th—"

"Should...we wait up for you?" Markov took a drag from his cigarette and let the smoke roll around in his mouth.

"Naw. Later."

"How late?" Mark asked softly.

"...not too late," Alex replied, wincing at his stinging eyes.

Markov smiled, then turned his back to the pair. He walked away from them, then sat down on one of the stools with the trio of Maloso.

They were soon talking again, gesturing wildly. Markov let out a bellowing laugh, and the table was slammed with a fist again.

Alex stood, then reached out his hand for Moira. After a moment's hesitation, she took it and stood. Moira looked at the back of the taller man's head and then at Al's face.

"...what?" he asked behind his shoulder, leading her to the door.

"You two are doing a horrible job," Moira replied, shuffling after him.

Alex held the door for Moira, and the two walked outside. The lights were bright. New York was the city that never sleeps, after all.

There was a small potted rose bush in bloom that Moira plucked a flower from as they passed by. She tucked her hair behind her ear and placed it there.

Alex shoved his hands in his pockets as he walked, still blinking wildly. Moira pulled her bag over her shoulder to clutch the strap.

"What do you mean by that?" he asked, over his shoulder.

"It's written all over your stupid faces. Those dumb shits will figure it out at some point," Moira said, and noticing he was pulling out a pack of cigarettes, continued, "give me a cigarette."

"You didn't let Markov give you one," he chided, "he always offers when he smokes."

"He's intimidating," she replied.

"And I'm not?" he asked, placing the cigarette between his lips.

"No. You're short, carajito. A pissed-off little dog," Moira said harmlessly.

Alex cracked a grin. Moira held her bag-strap tight against her chest.

He lit the cigarette and passed it to her. She stared at the cigarette for a few moments before putting it between her lips.

"Aren't you worried?" she asked, coughing from the smoke she inhaled.

"Definitely. Uncharted territory," he said, tilting his head to the side as he spoke, "See, clever. Like I said—"

"That's not what I meant," she replied, making the universal symbol for her next sentence, "you know."

"...what?" the blond responded, his eyes dancing between the rose in Moira's hair and her face.

"The news. What they're saying. You know," Moira was having trouble explaining herself, made worse by all the coughing.

"Ah. Ah, right. *That* news."

Alex bristled. He walked across the street without waiting for the light to change. Or waiting for her, for that matter. He cupped his cigarette as he walked, the lighter glowing orange and yellow in his hands. It bathed his face in gold.

"Um...Hey! Wait!" she yelled, shuffling after him on her sneakers. She flicked her cigarette to the street in her haste to chase him down. The rose behind her ear fell as she bolted forward; she heard the sound of shattering glass.

"What about that opportunity?" Moira pleaded. She looked back for the rose, but it was gone.

"I don't know what's wrong with the world right now. People, I guess," Alex ignored her question as he barreled forward.

"...what—"

"I've been nothing but kind to you, you maced me, you're prying at shit you shouldn't, and we've already—"

Alex halted once he hit the sidewalk, the smoke around his head filtering the light above. He faced her and rested his back against the post, arms crossed, eyes narrowed.

"It could happen! Hey! I don't know where you've been. I'm just—" Her fleeting words trailed off into the air like the ribbons of smoke peeling from his mouth.

"All I'm trying to do is help you," he said, exasperated, rubbing at his eye with his palm.

"...and I have no idea what you're trying to help me with!" she shot back in her defense.

"And where, *exactly*, do you think I've been?" The blond waved his cigarette in the air, punctuating his sentence.

"You're projecting! I didn't mean it like that!" Moira threw up her hands in frustration.

"Maybe I am, but..." Alex shifted his weight, head leaning back against the pole. He raised his chin and flicked his cigarette ash onto the street. His smile was serrated.

"Seguro que no eres un tremenda sata?" Moira was stunned by familiar words in his unfamiliar, devilish mouth.

"Fuck *you*, pendejo!" Moira shouted, preparing to slap the blond across the face. But his smile stopped her—he wanted her to hit him.

"No. How do you like insinuating fucking questions? Makes you feel like shit, huh?" Alex said, looking down his chin at Moira like she was nothing but a waste of space.

"...enough of this. You're not worth the fucking effort." Alex turned around and started to walk away.

"I was going to give you a way to get that bar. The bar we were just in. Like some fucking," Alex spit his cigarette out and onto the sidewalk, "fairy godmother bullshit, but you're just not clever enough."

"No...hey..." Moira pleaded, stumbling after Alex, who could've been an Olympic-level power-walker if that was even a real sport.

"I don't want to see you here again. And I don't want to get us in trouble," he said, slowing just enough so that Moira didn't miss his words.

"...you'd get in trouble? With your boss?" Moira was connecting the dots.

"He *is* my boss," spat the blond, who angled his brow in irritation.

"So keep your big mouth shut, or I will shut it for you. And you just lost a longtime fucking customer."

"...e-excuse me?" Moira stammered out.

"I wanted you to be the one to run the bar," Alex said, daunted. He flooded his hand over his mouth, rubbed his eyes, and pulled his fingers through his hair.

"I go to Rosalin's every Tuesday and Thursday. I have for the past two years. Best pizza I've had in my entire life. I don't expect you to remember everybody, but we've had this fucking conversation before, Moira..." he said, holding up his palm.

Moira scanned her memory, but the only thing she remembered was washing dishes and waiting tables. Could he be lying? She thought back, trying to piece the conversations together.

She thought back on the sink incident from earlier and screwed her eyes shut.

"...damn it..." she hissed, remembering a scrap of something. An opportunity, strictly business. Bad tourist shirt. An obnoxious blond guy. This obnoxious guy. All guys were obnoxious.

"You're smart, but you're just going through the motions. You also seem mostly fucking miserable," he said with a heavy sigh.

"You've...been spying on me?!" Moira asked, her voice shrill.

"It's my job to be very, very, very observant. Plus, Boris took a liking to you—which you don't remember—and I had to pull him away, which you also don't remember."

"I don't date gangsters..." Moira protested.

"You sure about that?" Silence.

"...don't come back here," Alex said.

"...alright."

"I don't want to see you here ever again."

"...alright."

But he did see her there every night for the next month. Standing at that corner, with her bag over her shoulder, the strap clutched in her hands, watching as he entered the bar with the taller man and the trio of idiots.

Sometimes it rained, and she still stood there, watching.

Waiting. Sometimes he'd bring a girl on his arm. Sometimes he'd bring no one. Sometimes he looked at her, and sometimes he didn't.

Moira stood in the snow this time, cold, leg-warmers pulled over her boots. She had her bag slung over her shoulder, wrapped tightly in a too-thin coat.

It was mid-day. The light was low; however, it was too early for the boys to go to the bar. Curiously, he'd still shown up with the taller man. It seemed they were grabbing coffee across the street, judging by their gesturing.

Moira shivered and looked on, wrapping her arms around herself to warm up. Her skin prickled, daunted by the frost. Alex stopped, said something to Markov, and then crossed the street when the light changed.

"...hey," Alex said, looking at anything but the dark-haired woman shivering in the cold.

"Hi," she replied, similarly not looking at him.

"Why..." Moira shivered, snow in her long, dark hair, "Why did you want me to have the bar?"

"Boris has it now. I don't like him. Neither does Mark, but we can't do much about it. He's dumb. And a man," Alex said, rocking back on his heels as snow dusted over his yellow hat.

"....yeah?" Moira looked over his face, trying to coax the words free.

"He took an interest in you. You're beautiful and very clever...at least I had hoped."

Moira scanned Alex's face, trying to understand what he was asking her to do. Realization dawned as a gust of wind whipped around her head.

"...what do I need to do?" she asked.

"Dress the part. Use what you have. Get him to sign it over," Alex said, wincing at the cold winds.

"You act like it's the easiest thing in the world...Do I have to, you know?" Moira, yet again, gestured as she had before.

"No, he's a lightweight. Just get him drunk and make a show of it," he paused, "I'd do it if he swung that way. I also can't use that trick on any of them. They know how I operate, and it'd end badly," the blond admitted, a distant look on his face.

"...he can't protect you?" Moira gestured with her chin at Markov across the street. He had an oversized jacket on, something obnoxious and denim, and a scarf wrapped up around his face; very European and hardly stylish.

"You...don't know a lot about where we come from, do you?" Alex asked, voice soft.

"No..." she admitted, shaking her head.

"In many parts of the world, if you're like me, you're either in a certain job, you keep it under wraps, or escape. Sometimes all three at different times," Alex said, accent underpinning his words, "Shit like this doesn't fly. We'd be too obvious if he played favorites any more than he already is. My leash is already very, very long."

"Oh..." she responded, looking over the blond's face. Every word he'd said seemed to take a lot out of him, and yet he'd said so very little.

"So, are you going to try?" he asked.

"I...don't even know you...why are you doing this?" she asked, snow dotting her long brown hair.

"Why have you been standing in this same spot for weeks?"

Alex paused for a moment and shifted his weight. He looked off to the side and stared at a trash can for a few seconds. He was staring through it, thinking. She could see the emotions flash across his face as he tried to find the words.

"I'm desperate. I need him crippled in any way I can."

"...but why?" Moira persisted, shivering in the cold.

"The minivan joke after you maced me...wasn't just a joke," Alex shifted his weight again and finally succumbed to the chill, "I've come a long...long fucking way. I can't pull the con again, and I need," Alex struggled with his words as if explaining this any further would conjure the worst into being, like a spell.

"I need it to *stop*," Alex hissed. He pulled down his yellow beanie and shivered.

"So...you're going to use me...to get it done," Moira said plainly.

"Yes. Yes. I am. And I'm not giving you another option."

Moira swiped snow out of her hair and looked over his pale face. He still wasn't meeting her gaze.

"You know too much. I'm using it as leverage," Alex said, finally drawing his intense blue stare to rest on her eyes. The smile she'd seen earlier returned, both beckoning and destructive.

"...so that's how it is," she said.

"That's how it is," he replied with a cheshire grin.

"You're ruthless," she said. Alex laughed.

Markov crossed the street on tall legs, walking swiftly as cars stopped for him. He hadn't bothered to wait for the light, and when a driver dared to honk, Mark shot him a gaze so red-hot it halted traffic itself.

"You don't know the half of it," Alex said behind chattering teeth. Al took off his hat abruptly and jammed it over Moira's dark curls.

"Ah! Hey…"

"You're cold. I don't need it. But I do need to meet with you later."

Markov had reached them by now and looked over the pair, most of his face obscured by his terrible scarf.

"…your boyfriend is, uh, blackmailing me," Moira said with an awkward smile.

"He's not my…" Markov started, but Alex shot him a look. It was death by a million cuts.

Alex looked away and zippered his jacket up higher, so it covered his mouth and nose.

"Tomorrow, here," he said to Moira through the fabric.

Alex tucked a piece of paper in her coat pocket and turned to leave. Markov followed after him. It was his turn to try to keep up. He was struggling with it, despite being so tall.

Moira took the piece of paper out of her pocket and held it between numb fingers.

"Ugh…it's going to take an hour to get there by train…" she said to herself before she rolled her eyes and groaned. Moira walked after the pair; she needed to cross the street anyways. With the paper between her fingers, she watched the two men and listened to them speak.

Markov trailed after Alex and finally caught up to him. They ordered coffee; brisk—they weren't staying. Now at the door, Alex looked back at Mark and spoke.

"I'm stepping out for a cigarette."

"Alright. I'll grab the coffee and meet you outside," Markov replied.

Alex headed out onto the sidewalk. He picked up the pace and didn't stop walking.

By the time Mark got the coffee, Alex was gone. He was left holding two searing cups in his hands. He peered around the corner and then looked off towards Moira, marching towards Rosalin's, past him.

"...did you see where he went?" Markov asked.

"...you are horrible at this," Moira said, fixing the yellow beanie on top of her head.

"Excuse me?" Markov pulled at the coffee's plastic lid with his mouth and managed to maneuver the cup to sip, "Ah, damn, it's boiling..." he said with a wince.

"...what am I getting myself into?" she asked, wrapping her arms around her chest.

"With him? No idea," Markov said, hovering over the burning coffee, "He's about as stable as a livewire shoved into a swimming pool." Markov tried again to take a sip but grimaced at the molten liquid.

"...what are you getting yourself into?" Moira asked, testing his reaction to her question.

"...I don't know. He's about as stable as a livewire shoved into a swimming pool."

Moira shoved her hands into her coat pocket and walked past Markov, who glanced at her. He followed her with his eyes as she walked. Moira didn't say goodbye and went towards Rosalin's.

Her shoes got stuck in some slush, and she stumbled. Soon, she realized she was going nowhere and fell back onto her rear as her feet flew out beneath her.

Her back landed directly on the hard surface. She let out a yelp. Disoriented, she looked around and found herself splayed onto the floor of a janitor's closet covered in cleaning solution.

"Fuck..." she muttered, holding her head as she took to sitting. The door opened wide, light blinding her. Diana gasped.

The person who was staring at her was the last person she wanted to see right now. Her heart pummeled like a trapped bird in the cage of her ribs as his shadow fell over her.

Alex raised his stolen laser rifle and squared up his body, moving forward to press it point blank into her forehead. His blue eyes spelled out just how much he wanted to blow her brains out.

"Get up."

She said nothing and pushed backward, steadying herself. She put out her hands in front of herself. Not that they'd protect her from a blast.

"Uh...Don't shoot."

"Walk forward," he said blankly.

Diana did as she was told, soap trailing off of her heels to the floor. She slipped a bit and steadied herself on his arm. He maneuvered the gun to point at her face again. She pulled away, eyes locked on its reticle.

"Walk." Alex shrugged her off of the weapon, and she moved to walk in front of him. He placed the head of the gun directly at the back of her skull and pressed. She flinched.

"...w-where are we going, pet?"

"Don't call me that. Forward." Alex bumped the gun into the back of her head.

"...I remembered something...something strange, not unlike a memory. We were at a bar..." she tried to make conversation as he led her through the killing floor. She stepped over bodies—blood was everywhere.

Maya was standing by a door, peering beyond it. She didn't seem to care about the carnage.

"We're all clear, but there's prolly more comin'," the shorter woman said over her shoulder.

"Gotcha," Alex said.

"I remembered when we met, before…" Diana tried again.

"Congratu-fucking-lations. You were a bitch then and a bitch now." Alex pushed her forward with the gun. She flinched, scraping forward on heels.

"W-where are we going, dea—where are we going?" Diana stammered.

"I taught you too well. And now you don't know how to turn it off."

"…pardon?"

Maya burst through a door, and Alex shoved Diana forward. Once inside, the trio scoured the room. They'd have to crawl through a shaft to escape, it seemed. Maya was working on ripping the grate out of the wall to do just that.

"…it's like you forgot how to be a person," Alex said, his accent peeking through the words.

"You just left her there and hid in a closet. You made no fucking moves to do jack or shit. The fuck is wrong with you?" Alex wasn't waiting for an answer. Instead, he tore the grate open with one hand, the metal twisting. He tossed it aside, and Maya crawled in first.

"…how far does this go down, do ya think?" asked Maya, lingering at the entrance.

"We need to get to Polly and Henry—shit's goin' down. I think my schematics are accurate, but I'm not sure since

I've been fucking cut off. We're going to have a problem with the drop, though," he said through grit teeth. Maya climbed through the vent, the gun holstered in the back of her pants.

"...what sort of problem?" Diana asked before Alex shoved her into the vent with a kick. She knocked her head on the top of it with a clank and winced.

"Ow..."

"Forward." Alex pushed her onwards as she crawled on soap-slicked hands and knees.

"Uh...*yeah*, we're gonna' have a 'problem' with tha drop...it's 4 bajillion feet down," Maya said, her voice reverberating against the metal. She sounded like she was in a wind tunnel.

"What does it land on?" he asked.

"....I think it's...clothes?" Maya responded, a little louder this time.

"Do we risk it?" asked the blond in a softer voice than he'd used before.

"...we gotta, right? Shoulda had Di take up the front so we coulda landed on her," Maya said with a snort. Diana remained silent, but her heartbeat was louder than ever.

"Alright. It's now or never. Liv."

"Right." Maya didn't correct him and popped down the shaft. Air whipped around her face. Thankfully she was right and fell on a pile of what looked to be laundry. But it was a far enough drop that she rolled off of it and banged herself into an old machine with a metallic popping sound.

Diana came next, and as she fell, she screeched. She landed more gracefully.

"..are you all right, dear?" Diana asked, steadying herself to stand.

"Funny that yer askin' that now," Maya hissed, standing on unsure footing.

Alex landed on the laundry pile and more or less fell right through it into the concrete. He landed on his feet, the weight of his metallic body surging up through his fake joints and bones. The floor cracked.

He didn't skip a beat and held up the rifle again at Diana's head.

"Where are we." It was a statement, not a question. Maya looked at the antique machinery and opened up one of the washers.

"...This is all super old..." Maya said, "this is wicked weird..."

"It must have been left over from when they came up here..." Diana said, eyeing Alex's laser rifle as it was now trailing to her eye. It was a few centimeters shy of pressing into it.

"That doesn't make any sense. Why would they have old washers and dryers?" Alex looked around at the antique machinery, "...does anyone know about this place?"

"No, not that I know of, dear..." Diana said nervously.

She raised her hands and turned around so he could press the gun to the back of her head.

"...How far down are we?" Alex asked.

"I think we have one more floor, d-dear. But I'm not sure."

"Alright. Let's find a way down," the blond said, "and Diana," he continued as he pressed her forward with his laser gun. It'd sear a hole straight through her, cauterizing the wound as it did so. She'd die almost instantly.

Knowing him, he'd make it last longer. Shoot her in the

shoulder, maybe blast off her arm and heat it so she'd have to live with the damage.

"Y-yes?"

"If you fuck us over again, I'm putting a bullet in you."

"...I know."

"Good, so we're all on the same page, then."

"I have to ask," she began, her voice hesitant.

"What? What do you 'have' to ask?" Alex spat, hardly gentle.

"Who died and made you God?" Diana sneered, although Alex couldn't see it.

Maya walked towards her and glared up at her.

"Who made ya' such a coward?" Maya was about to spring into a tirade, but Alex stopped her with a glance.

"We don't have time for this. Let's find a way out. We need to meet up with them. Hopefully, they're not fucking dead," Alex settled the matter.

Maya took up the front to prepare against attackers, and at some point, Alex took up the rear.

At some point, they had even given Diana a gun.

And at some point, she hoped they would forgive her.

"WE ARE NOT ANYWHERE near the fucking Greens," Alex spat, "How the fuck did we end up going...up?" Red light bathed his face in the color of war, poppies, and painted lips.

Old saloon-styled buildings flooded from the ground like fence posts. In between them lived brick buildings far taller than the eye could see. Smog hung in the air and obscured the upper floors. Toxic smoke sat near the ground and covered the dirt roads. Asphalt bled in patches over the earth.

The building directly in front of the trio had a flashing neon sign with a naked woman in fluorescent lights. Next to her were letters that spelled out the word D.I.V.A. The symbol of the woman flickered between standing, kneeling, then rolled down to squat spread eagle.

"...We're...in The Reds?" Alex hissed his question as Diana made an equally irritated sound, more dismay than his irritation. She raised her gun; they had given her the smallest one, yet it was curiously equipped with a dimmer, hinting at its hidden power.

"Ya...I guess?" Olive chimed in, turning up her nose at the place.

"I've heard stories, dears...this isn't a place we want to stay in for long," Diana replied, squinting through the red light that threatened to blind her. Her weapon was readied, for what, she wasn't yet sure.

"This place..." Alex's words died in his throat.

Maya shot him a look which he deftly avoided, and then she looked off into the distance for a bit too long. Something was pulling at her peripherals, just like the stack of vinyl records in her earlier flashback.

"What about Hen an' Polly?" Maya asked, narrowing her eyes at all the red beyond them.

"I don't know, princess. Can't link up; Tyr made sure I was neutered."

"...uh.." Diana drawled.

"From the network. Di, get your head out of the gutter," Alex spat.

"Speaking of which...darling, just what had you been doing while we were accosted?" asked Diana.

"None of your fucking," Alex turned around a corner with his weapon raised. Nothing but trash and a passed-out guy that smelled like puke, "business."

The guy had a mustard-colored hat on and a purple coat. He had sunglasses on his head with numbers attached to the top of the dark lenses. Souvenir glasses, caked in glitter. Familiar; something from a different time.

Alex held his breath and took the glasses off the man's face. The man didn't stir. He was either dead or so drunk he couldn't function.

"...the fuck?" Alex asked, turning them over in his hands.

"What?" Maya asked.

"These..." Alex responded, holding up the glasses. Maya walked over and plucked them from his fingers.

"Creepy." Maya said. She held them in her hands, examining the details. Glitter came off and stuck to her skin. She flicked her fingers, sending tiny shards of colorful light into the air.

As the glitter was cast, she stared off again, distracted by something unseen beyond all the red.

"Yeah...very creepy..." Alex wiped glitter off onto his pants. Maya pocketed the glasses.

The trio moved onwards through the street. Every now and then, a gaggle of well-dressed men walked by. Sometimes, a murder of well-dressed women. Alex assumed they didn't want anyone to know they were here, and of course, he was right.

Alex saw a pair of well-dressed men dragging a woman who walked on unsteady footing.

"....the fuck is this shit?" Alex grimaced, "Don't tell me it's—"

"Didn't ya download schematics of tha ship when you were hooked up?" Maya asked, grimacing as she watched the girl being dragged like livestock.

"I did, but it didn't tell me that this shit was going down..." Alex trailed off, then sneered, "different fucking time, same fucking problems. I guess we never..." the words died. He had a mission to enact, one born in the blood.

Alex raised his weapon and was about to stalk towards the two men and do what he did best. Maya grabbed his shirt sleeve. He stopped when she tugged him back.

"We don't have tha time fer this. Not right now," Maya said, freezing Alex in place.

"...she's tied up like an *animal*," he protested, gesturing with his weapon.

"Darling, we either save her and get caught and all of this was for nothing, or we do what we need to, and she gets saved later," Diana chimed in.

"I can't just—" The words spat from his mouth like stunted bullets.

"Dear, we have to go. This isn't our fight, not right now." Alex bristled as Diana placed a hand on his shoulder, "Love, we need to get out of here. It's not safe."

Alex reluctantly agreed. The three of them holstered their weapons. The femme fatale tried to figure out where to put hers. She only had a small pocket where she had placed the sticker. The gun wouldn't fit, so she stuck it the only place it would—squarely between her breasts.

Maya gave her a look.

"I don't have pockets!" Diana shouted. Alex flashed a smirk. It fell as he watched the woman being carted away again. The back of her body was made of gutted wires and nothing more.

"God damn it," he said to himself. The synth chattel stumbled. Alex's face fell further. This was too familiar, and he would never not hate the theft of agency.

The trio walked into the large building. Alex noticed a barcode reader at the front of it. A bouncer stood and looked him over. Their eyes connected.

"You tell anyone we're here, and I'll rip out your—"

"Cash, sir. Credits. Don't ask, don't tell," the man said roughly, interrupting him.

"...How much?" Alex asked, a hand on his hip.

"20 mil. I won't say nothin'."

"...Seriously?" Maya gawked, "that's enough ta' buy yer own plot on—"

Diana pushed past Alex. He shot her a look. She swiped her wrist over the barcode reader. A small bleep signaled the transaction's success. The bouncer grinned.

"They didn't cut you off?" Alex asked, narrowing his eyes.

"There's a reason I didn't save the princess," Diana said, "I *did* have a plan, you know," she added with a smirk, "how could you ever doubt me?" she continued, ending on a cheshire grin. Alex rolled his eyes at her and ushered the trio forward with a vague gesture.

The lights were far too bright in this gyrating hellscape. The smells were too intense. Everything had come at Alex all at once, and all of it competed for his highly tuned attention. Alex's sensors started to stream streaks of color and haptic readings. They tumbled on each other, glitch-like.

It was like when he monitored his friends' actions, took their various readings, and played back loops, only throttled up to eleven.

Alex was full of nothing but sensations in this moment, eyes screwed shut, and head ducked down to avoid even the very air itself. Each flashing light burned his eyes. Every smell, every sound, every color—

"Close it down. Focus on one thing," a voice caught his attention. Alex cracked open one eye, which was a feat in all this deluge of sensory input.

Sitting at a booth was someone they didn't recognize; a young man with his legs neatly crossed. In his hand was an ordinary shot glass.

"Too much, right? The sounds, the people. Bet you're

seeing night vision and all sorts of nasty heat signatures. It's like being on molly. Almost. Sort of."

"Molly?" He hadn't heard that term in a while. Alex wove around a woman with a snake around her shoulders, a woman in pastel yellow, and a man in black, to sidle beside this stranger.

The two women followed suit. Maya sat across from the stranger, and Diana sat beside her.

The stranger sat back with that token satiated look Alex gave when he wanted to rip someone's throat out with his teeth. Except it didn't seem nearly as deadly; heady confidence, not heady evisceration.

Maya unholstered her pistol and placed it directly at the stranger's kneecap.

"There's no need for that, Olive," the young man said.

"The *fuck* did you just call her?" It was Alex's turn to raise his weapon.

Alex looked over this stranger's features. He didn't recognize them. His brows were pale, his eyes far too large for his face. Brown-haired and almost gaunt-looking. He was young—couldn't have been over nineteen or twenty. Maybe. Maybe he was just youthful-looking, like Tyr.

Designed to be something he wasn't, like a lie within a lie.

But the youth's heartbeat was stable, this he read—he could still do that at least, despite Tyr's tampering. Stable, and he was unusually warm.

"I'm still drinking. I know you don't like that, but it's hard to quit."

Alex screwed his brows together and burned daggers into the stranger's face, scanning for something. A memory, a scrap of information, a spark of an idea. Fucking anything.

"...Moira still likes that color, I guess. Your favorite, too, right? At least she didn't mace you in the face this ti–" Alex flicked the laser rifle on. It hummed to attention. He pressed the rifle deep into the young man's temple.

Silence fell upon them all. Alex's senses no longer screamed with what was outside, for he had focus. One solitary spot of agony to affix on. Now, the torturous sensations would come from within.

The realization was slow, like woken from sleep, or perhaps the yawning of a cello.

At first, there was terror tugging at the blond's eyebrows. The cautious murmur of fright flickered to a crescendo of disbelief. It was replaced with violent joy, joy like Maya had never seen on his face before. Then confusion, a fuzzy deliriousness.

Then came pain.

Undiluted wreckage broke across the blond's face. Death by a thousand cuts flickered in the blue of his eyes. He was black water personified, a metal husk filled with liquefied loss, boiled down to his bare metal bones. Alex's vibrant personality had been swept away, deleted, forgotten. He had been unmade.

His expression fell as his weapon followed suit. Black no longer, Alex became blank.

"Got your face done?" asked the stranger, idling with his shot glass.

"...Yes."

"Good. This look suits you," the stranger knocked back a shot, "Inked up again, huh? Still have the flowers?"

"...Poppies," Alex's words were glass, broken between his teeth. They cut him all the same, but this stranger's voice was far worse. Every single syllable was a stab between his ribs.

"Yes. I liked those the most."

Maya looked at the two of them, made a face, then jerked her head to the crowd. Her gaze was distant. It wasn't until Diana half-asked a very important, very short question that Maya pried her hazel eyes back to the events at hand.

"Maloso? No way," Diana blurted out, leaning forward, "Um...how did you get here? Why do you look—"

"Yeah, we all look tha same..." Maya finished Diana's sentence for her. Maya became quiet, her expression growing pained with each passing moment. She wasn't looking at Alex. She was looking through him.

"Darling, what do you keep looking at?" Maya ignored Diana's question. Diana angled her head to look at the shorter woman's face.

"Dear?" Diana tried again. Maya wouldn't answer her. Instead, Maya sat back, deflating as the moments passed, as if sinking into the sofa of yore.

Alex placed his gun on the table before sitting in the booth; it drew Maya's attention. The stranger looked over Alex's face. Alex didn't look back. He stared directly ahead and took in nothing.

"I'm not sure. Maybe it's an error. Maybe it's purposeful," the stranger finally replied.

"But you...know who you are, yes? You remember, pet? I remember. Did you start remembering recently, dear?" Diana asked, crossing her arms and leaning back in her seat. She flicked her gaze to Maya's round face. She was getting nothing from Maya.

Diana looked to Alex; similarly, he gave her nothing.

"The ideas just kept coming a year or so back. Thought I

was going crazy," the youthful stranger admitted. He smiled, swiped another shot off the table, and knocked it back into his throat.

"But then I saw what was on that ancient dossier...it was all true."

Diana raised a brow, trying to grasp her friends' attention with a glance, yet Maya still avoided her.

Sebastian opened his mouth to continue, but Alex interrupted him.

"You. Where," his pause was an expanse as wide as the sea of stars, "have you been?"

"...Here. I'm Sebastian now. And shorter. Much shorter," Sebastian laughed. He shot Alex a smile that pierced his guts. Alex bolted instinctively.

Sebastian tried to grab his shirt as Maya stood up with a start, but it was no use. Diana shouted after him, but he was gone.

The synth was far too fast.

He ran out into the street with the red signs and booked it down the dirt and over the asphalt. He ran as he had from Tyr, but faster. He ran as Maya had run from the guards, but faster. He ran as Polly and Henry had run from the giant mechanized war machine that had seared a hole through the wheat field, but faster. He had to outrun this, though he knew he could never.

Alex stumbled over a trash can as he tried to sweep up a littered alley-way.

Every step spelled one thing and one thing only: that smile had been what truly killed him, and something in his core knew it enough to spur the synth to run for his fucking life.

THE CONVERSATION HAD CONTINUED without Alex. The three had agreed he needed to process this on his own, without commenting on the matter. However, Diana was restless.

"...We found this," Maya said as she pushed the glittered glasses towards Sebastian. The man smiled and picked them up, dusting some of the glitter off onto the table.

"What is it?" Maya asked, leaning forward to look at the cast-off glitter

"I put it there. He's forgetting a lot. I think I'm supposed to make him remember," Sebastian said softly.

"...Are you, pet?" Diana asked as she grabbed Sebastian's drink from the table and knocked it into the back of her throat, "Ugh, what is this vile filth?" she grimaced, obviously regretting her decision.

"Vodka," Sebastian said with a dry smile.

"...How stereotypical," Diana uttered underneath her breath. Abruptly, she lurched to attention. She pulled out the 'symbol' she'd found in the library and placed it on the table, pushing it towards the stranger.

"The little one and I found this too," Diana cooed, proud of herself, casting a quick glance at the door as if looking for the obnoxious tourist shirt of old. Diana's face fell, her pride dashed just as quickly as it had come on.

"It's a trigger. I need him to remember," Sebastian said, seemingly only firm in that fact.

"A...trigger..." Diana whispered under her breath. She stole a glance across the room.

"Why?" Maya asked, finally putting her gun back where it belonged. Her expression was less unfocused than earlier but still full of conflict.

"I don't know," Sebastian said, "I only know that he needs to know. All of you do." Maya nodded at his response; she agreed.

"While you two discuss this...madness...I," Diana twisted in her seat, peering beyond the booth, "I need to check in on him," Diana looked down at Maya, expectantly urging her out of the way, "Pet. I need to."

Maya nodded solemnly, shifting out of the seat to let her pass. Diana, once freed, ran much like Alex had, yet not nearly as fast.

In the red streets, Alex tripped over a trash can and ricocheted to the ground. He couldn't outrun this wound. It wouldn't let him. He'd have to let it bleed out from the back of his skull. He wanted anything but that because it meant he'd have to see it, feel it, and hear it.

Now sitting, he grabbed the sides of his head and drew in gasping breaths. Truth loomed, encased in blistering metal, first led by a sight, then a sound, then a drive, and finally, a gun.

This was something more painful than any wound he'd

suffered, and he had certainly suffered more injuries than he'd ever shared with the others.

It was even more painful than knowing, and not knowing, what Tyr had done to him.

Because this pain came from someone he had loved.

THE CLUB WAS alight with youths flowing like cells, multiplying and separating in time with organic movement. A band guided their symphony. Song became action. Movement. Life itself.

Waves of orange and gold painted the singer's dark skin. The light bounced off of the piercing that hooked from her ear to her nose in a silver wire. Her thin jewels commanded attention.

Alex took a bright green drink and dripped some of the contents onto a woman's navel, who was lying on a long table. She laughed as he licked the salt from her thigh and sucked the alcohol from her stomach.

She went to grab his face, but he moved away.

"Sorry. I'm just window-shopping. I only buy," the blond tipped the rest of his alcohol down his throat, "one thing at a time."

The blond spun around and lifted his hands up as he crooned. Eric came up behind him and slapped his hands over his shoulders.

"Mate, this is tha best fuckin' party ever!"

"Fuck yes it is...hey, Erica," Alex teased, his pet name for Eric drawn out far past the point of sobriety.

"That girl's pretty cute, huh?" the blond reeled, gesturing vaguely at a yellow and magenta shape in the corner of the room.

"Totally...ey...wait. Why're ya askin' me that?" Eric squinted at the yellow shape. Percy came into focus.

"She keeps," Alex tried to force his vision to cooperate, yet he could only make out vague lines and colors, "..makin' eyes at you..." the blond gestured with a floating, slowed hand, "and doing that thing with a cherry, you...know the thing. It's red, so...it's probably. With. Yeah."

"....mate, she's taken," Eric dipped as Alex swayed to his arm. Alex started to chuckle, face rosy, already growing far too snug into his taller friend's chest.

"Where's...Ollie?" Eric asked. It was Eric's turn to try to stabilize himself on the shorter man who was laughing against his chest.

"...Who?" Alex narrowed his blurry eyes before snorting in hysterics, "Aubrey?" Alex couldn't seem to hold himself up, but he did his best to swerve his head around looking for this unknown friend.

"One of Liv's coffee buddies!" Alex screamed into the crowd around them. Eric tried to keep Alex level, but he also wasn't in the best shape, either. Alex laughed into his hand and reeled around the crowded club for Markov. He didn't see him.

Eric and the yellow shape were forgotten. Alex stumbled onwards, with no apparent direction. Lost, as he was always lost.

"Goddd, I know I'm not fucking supposed to...but, mm," Alex tilted his foggy head to the side, "we should dance...even once. Just one dance. Nobody has to know...we could be fuckin' anybody..."

Alex took out his pager and paged his not-boyfriend.

"Hmm. That....fucker could sleep through a damned...er...English. Alex, English. Торнадо. Fuck...ahh whatever," Alex had devolved beyond the point of real words. Now it was a mangling of his native tongue, English, and adopted languages he was far better at speaking than he had any business being.

Realizing in a stroke of impulsive genius that he wanted a cigarette, he stumbled for the door.

Now in the cool air, his pale blond hair was strewn around his head. He attempted to smooth it down, but his fingers were not cooperating in the slightest.

A pink shape greeted him. A pink shape that he remembered didn't drink, as it was getting late for her. Of course, she'd be out here, waiting until they drank themselves stupid enough to regret it, and she'd have to get them home.

"Hey, Liv, Livvie, Olivia," Alex dribbled out his words. He planted his ass right down next to her with an ungraceful thud. He lit up a cigarette and leaned closer to her. Too close, but she didn't shrink back.

"Hey!" Olive chirped happily, taking the headphones out of her ears. The music was as loud and bright as she was.

"Have you seen the guy with the great ass?" Alex started up, cackling himself stupid.

"Oh. Mark? Yeah. He got in the car with...you?" Olivia scrunched up her nose.

"...Fucking...pardon?" Alex stared at her like she had grown a second head.

"Yeah. Thought it was you, but I wasn't sure." Olivia

said, pulling down her headphones and placing her Walkman in her coat pocket.

"...how weren't you sure?" Alex was starting to sober up, his gaze drilling through her face.

"I dunno'. They had a big coat and hat on, and um..." Olivia scrunched up her nose and then looked at his face, "...I thought it was you...'cause they were real handsy..."

Alex shot up and stumbled with his back onto the brick wall. He felt like he was going to puke.

"His car?" he barked out his question.

"Yer car," Olive said with a tiny grimace on her face.

"My car?!" Alex screeched. Olive winced.

"....what...the....*fuck!*" the blond roared louder than a war-cry.

Alex bolted forward to make a break for Mark's car, but he didn't have the keys, and he was too fucked up to think straight. Toppling into a trash can, he instead took to kicking it repeatedly while swearing in a language Olive assumed was Russian. It didn't sound like it, though.

"...are ya speakin' drunkanese?" Olive asked, standing up slowly. Alex made another dash but found himself with his hands to his knees, staggering.

"Hey! Yer too drunk ta think clearly, let alone drive— hey!" Olive ran up behind him and grabbed him by the belt loop, and yanked. Alex stumbled into her.

"Lemme' drive. Ya got keys?" Olive insisted, her small grabby palm open and waiting.

"Fuck no, I don't 'got keys'..." he spat, against his better wishes.

"What about Eric's car? Ya got his keys?" she chirped back. A long time passed before he said anything.

"No," he whimpered, twisting to curl his face to his

shoulder, hands still on his knees, looking like he was about to start sobbing at any moment. Olive held up her hands.

"Gosh, didn't take ya fer a weepy drunk. Ok. I got this. I got this. I'll get his keys, and I'll drive ya'. Okay?" Alex said nothing.

"Okay?" she repeated, harsher than she had last time.

"Ok," Alex whimpered.

Olivia burst back into the club and launched at Eric. She noticed he was talking to Percy but paid it no mind and slipped her hand into his pocket. Ripping out his keys, Eric swiveled to grab at her, but she was too fast.

"Oy! Oy! Hey! Pepto—goddamn it…"

"So…why do we need to play by the rules, hmm?"

Olivia rounded the pair of them and then burst out of the club to find Alex hunched over a trash can. His fingers were knuckle-white around the metal rim.

"Ew, are ya gonna ralph?" She scrunched up her nose in disgust.

"Already did," he gasped out, before making another disgusting retching sound.

"Gross. That's why I don't drink much. I jus' eat treats…"

"Yes, but if you eat too much," Alex heaved, hand struck out as if to stop her from judging him, "You get sick anyways…like the," Alex hesitated in between dry heaves, the words scattered like petals in the wind, "pixie stick incident," he proceeded to heave.

"Yuck, don't remind me…ugh…ya need water?"

"….yeah. Yeah."

Olive opened her bag and pulled out a bottle of water, and thrust it into his hands. He took it from her.

"You're…well…prepared…" he spoke between heaves, braced against the trash can.

"Course! Y'all get crazy at parties. Someone's gotta play babysitter."

Alex cracked a grin and opened the bottle of water with concentrated effort. He poured it into his mouth and then spit into the trash can. Once he was sure the puke was out of his mouth, he began to drink it down.

"Mm...thanks, Liv."

"No problemo. Now, let's get ya back home...or are ya gonna go to—"

"If he's fuckin' around, I'm...gonna' shoot him in the face..." the blond slurred out his threat of death.

"No, no hey...let's get ya home..." she held up her hands, trying to soothe the situation.

"No. Drive me to his flat," Alex insisted, his breathing uneven.

"...I don' think that's tha best idea, *dude*," Olive muttered.

"Don't 'dude' me, Olive. Get me—there," Alex gestured vaguely in a random direction. Olive stared at his outstretched arm and let out a deep sigh.

"If I don't drive ya, yer gonna try ta walk, huh?" Olivia asked, thin brow raising.

"Yeah," Alex said.

"...and if you walk, yer prolly gonna pass out in a dumpster, huh?"

"Yeah."

Olivia sighed deeply. Alex continued to drink down the water until it was gone. When he finished it, he tossed the empty bottle in the trash can. Olive took that moment to grab his hand.

"Fine. But if ya do somethin' stupid, I'm gonna have to stop ya," Olive said. Alex didn't reply.

They made their way to Eric's new car, which was a piece of shit, and too tall for Olive. She unlocked it, opened the door, and wiggled up onto the seat. Alex stumbled into it and almost slammed the door on his leg.

"Agh fuck!" he blurted out, immediately angry at the door and wishing death upon every door that ever existed.

"Be careful, you big stupid idiot!" she scolded him as he poured himself inside the vehicle.

"Sorry..." Alex's head fell back on the seat, eyes glassy and expression distant. Olivia took to starting up the car, but it retched just like he had until finally, it kicked into gear.

"Ok. Where we goin'?" He wasn't responding to her; instead, his head was lulling against the seat like lapping waves.

"...the address? Oh fuck damn...uh..." he drawled, screwing his eyes shut.

Olive held out her hand to gesture, "...landmarks. C'mon!"

"Penny's Jewelers up the street, hang a...left? Then we sweep up, uh..." Alex rubbed his eye raw with the palm of his hand.

"Go through the SoHo district past the drug store, then left up towards..." he motioned with a lazy, heavy gesture, "the...place...with all the...rich shit in it."

"Oh, he lives in tha swanky neighborhood with the giant trees n' crap?"

"Yeah. Swanky. Drivin' around with my pink chevy that-fuckingdouchepiece of shi—" Alex wasn't speaking words anymore; he was firing approximations of words in multiple languages.

As they drove, Alex hung his hand out the window and smoked. When they stopped at a light, Olive looked over at him. He was alternating between biting his nails and smoking.

He looked smaller than her, scrunched up in that seat, dwindling like the last dying leaf on a tree that should have been cut down long ago. Olive sighed, as if she'd seen this coming all along. Which she possibly had.

"Hey. How ya doin?" Olive asked, her voice soft.

"...how do you think I'm doing?" Alex spat against his better judgment.

"It coulda been nothin'. I coulda jus' been seein' stuff," Olive tried to reassure the blond.

"Olive. If you saw something, you saw it. You're the smart one," he said, looking up from his nail-biting at the girl in the driver's seat.

"...huh?" she asked, raising a thin brow.

"Everyone freaks out all the time. You keep a cool head. I just...try to punch people. You're the only one who's got their shit together..." Alex pressed the cigarette to his mouth like a blunt and held it there, smoke filling up Eric's car.

"...I play SNES in my jams on my days off..." she protested, turning a corner as gently as she could, but it wasn't gentle enough for Alex. He winced, hand now braced against the dashboard.

"Yeah, you also work a real-person job and hustle like a motherfucker," he added, his head spinning as they turned more corners.

"...I have pink hair, and my diet is sugar plus more sugar..."

"And you're the only one not sloshed tonight. That fuck-ing...means...something," he felt sick again and held back the retching of his stomach with a shaky hand.

Olivia quirked a smile and puffed up her feathers. He

noticed her filling with self-confidence and gave her a foggy grin. That is until he noticed his pink chevy.

"Hey! Stop! Right here!" he roared.

Olive throttled the brakes. Alex pressed one hand to the dashboard so he wouldn't smash his head. The other was reserved for acting as a second seatbelt for his diminutive driver.

"Pull 'round back, I'm coming up...the stairwell..." Alex garbled out.

"Do ya think that's a good idea? What if you fall..." Olivia warned the blond.

"I won't fuckin' fall," he protested, barely sitting in his seat as it was.

"Are ya sure...?" she questioned, both brows tilting up.

"When I was younger, I stole a lot of shit," the blond held up his hand as he explained, "One night, I got too tanked and tried to steal a vending machine. Managed to do it with some complicated pulley system and counterweights, a shopping cart, and some fucking cinder blocks."

Olive's eyes grew wide as she drove behind the back and put the vehicle in park.

"The moral of the story is that I can do anything drunk that I can do sober. Except, with more vomit, I guess," finishing his trip down memory lane with a shrug.

The car stopped humming. Olive placed the keys in her pocket and looked at the side of his face. He said nothing. He was psyching himself up for this. She noticed.

"Alex—"

With that, he jerked the door open and dropped out of the car. Finishing up his cigarette, he flicked it to the ground and ashed it under his boot. Olive rounded out of the vehicle, but not before making sure she locked it.

She walked over to him and stared up at the grated stairs that lead to the top floor.

"Uh...I dunno if I can make that," she said.

"You'll be fine. It's super easy."

Climbing the ladders and subsequent stairs would be 'super easy' as the blond wonder had said. What wouldn't be, however, was extracting him from the events that would follow. The events that marked him for life, and like all trauma, would never let him go.

In this case, it would never let her go, either.

ALEX TOOK a metal rod with a cinch on it and hooked it on the last rung of the rusted ladder before them. He pulled, and it came down fluidly. Olive took the lead—Alex had insisted. Any stumble on that ladder was met with him bracing her to help her climb.

"See, there're just stairs now..." Alex said.

"Y-yeah..." Olivia said. As they traversed the steps, she went behind Alex. As they neared the top floor, they heard music through the glass. "Voices Carry" by 'Til Tuesday was blasting far louder than it needed to.

"That's my fucking mixtape," the blond hissed.

Alex narrowed his brows and reached underneath the window to pull it up as quietly as he could. Olive's eyes widened.

"You've done this before, huh..."

Alex didn't answer her. He stepped inside, then offered her his hand. He guided her over the threshold of a disastrous idea. She let him.

"Oh, I love this song," she blurted out, far too loud for this delicate, delicate situation.

"Shh!" Alex hissed, and Olive held her mouth.

"Sorry," she whispered through her small fingers.

Olive looked around the living room. The floors were slick marble with gold, pink, and gray swirls. The curtains were patterned in dark damasks.

"Someone read tha Vampire Chronicles too much…" In fact, Olive found the very first book in the series on the table. She leafed through it.

"He's Euro Trash. What did you expect?" Alex snorted. Olivia placed the book back where she found it.

The blond took her hand in his own. It was warm, if a bit clammy.

There were countless books on countless bookshelves; some Markov didn't seem the type to read, many of which had brightly colored leaflets sticking from the pages. Some of the furniture didn't look like it fit the overall aesthetic, either.

It was then that Olive spotted Alex's favorite ashtray on a garish obsidian coffee table. It was pink yarrow with color-block shapes all over it.

Olive noticed a stack of cassette tapes and moved towards them. She lost Alex's grasp. As she thumbed through the cassettes, her eyes widened.

"You've all but moved in, huh…" she marveled, her hazel eyes creeping through the things she knew were his.

"Yes, now be quiet," Alex said in a hushed voice as he rounded to her side.

"Is that my fucking Prince record?! I didn't bring this over here…"

"Shh!" It was Olive's turn to shush him. Alex smirked and looked back at her.

They moved through to a hallway, and Alex held her little

paw in his hand. Olive passed by another shelf and played her little fingers over a stack of records. His posters were all over the walls. A painting Olive had made was framed near them.

"Oh! Ya kept it..." she said with a warm smile.

"Of course I kept it—hey! Shh."

Alex saw the bedroom door was ajar, the smallest sliver of light coming through it. He looked back at Olive and held the lifeline of her hand tight.

"...Are you sure you wanna do this?" she asked. Alex, however, didn't say a word.

Olive looked up at his face. She had never seen him terrified; she didn't think he was capable of that. Alex swallowed hard.

He reluctantly let go of her hand.

Alex kicked the door open with his foot. It slapped back on its hinges. Olive was startled by his immediate response; no more than mere moments ago, he'd been a stumbling, puking mess.

Alex was no longer drunk. If adrenaline could spark a man to sobriety, that was what it had done for him. Alex looked on as he saw someone strewn upon familiar, violently colorful sheets.

That someone was a woman, one he'd never seen before. Markov was pressed against her, and as stupid as Eric was, even he would've known what was going on. A fucking duck would've known what was happening.

"This isn't what it looks like," Markov said, expression flattening.

Alex rounded on his feet and bent to pick up a pencil from the floor. Then he began to pace.

"Uh...should I—" said the woman with her hand on the

headboard, obviously uncomfortable. Markov still had one of her red ponytails in his fist.

"Oh man, yer so screwed…" Olive said with her hands over her mouth. As if speaking it would manifest the violence like a spell.

Alex circled like a beast. When he'd rounded one end of the bed, he came back with a small turn. He held the pencil in one hand and ran his fingers through his hair. Gripped, held the back of his head, pulled. He was fidgeting, not looking at Markov, the girl, nor Olivia.

His actions were thoughts; he moved in order to think.

Alex turned to glare at Markov as he stalked. He swallowed hard, his jaw clenched, and he almost spoke. Almost, but he stopped himself.

"…We need to talk about this," Markov said in a tender voice. Alex said nothing and spun the pencil between his fingers.

"I didn't think we were exclusive." The pencil spun faster.

"…Who's this guy?" the woman asked. She tried to push back off the headboard but failed.

"Al. Alex. Hey, Al." Markov pulled away from the woman. The woman wrapped Alex's sheets around her body, shifted off of the bed, and started to get dressed in a hurry. Olive mouthed the word 'go.' She nodded, thankful, and quickly saw herself out.

"I told you what would happen if you fucked around, and yet, and yet, and fucking yet—"

The pencil spun faster in Alex's grip as Markov made the mistake of raising out his flat palm to the blond to stop the inevitable. There was a great deal of kinetic energy in that spinning pencil, and Markov wasn't ignorant to what the blond was capable of.

He was, however, ignorant enough to make a mere motion in his direction. After all, Alex was no prey animal. He was an apex predator. An apex predator that was feeling threatened because he'd just been emotionally gored in two.

Olivia, sensing what was about to happen, rushed Alex to grab his arm. She missed him, stumbling.

Markov leaned his weight to dodge whatever was coming his way. He had the benefit of being taller and stronger, but Alex was faster.

He was always faster.

Alex stepped the opposite way, and in one swoop, he ripped at Markov's hair, slammed his head down onto his slim knee, and then popped his skull off the bedpost with a sickening sound.

Olive rose to her feet, dazed. Her hazel eyes flickered over the scene playing out before her. Alex felt her eyes on him and bristled.

"You ignorant piece of shit. You. You, of all people, knew *better*," Alex bellowed, bolting towards Mark with the intent to take him out. Now on his knees, reeling from the attack, Markov could only defend himself.

Alex let Markov's arm pass by and jabbed his elbow down into the muscle as hard as he could. In a flash, Al had rounded behind him, pencil pressing into his jugular. Markov had only made it easier by kneeling.

"You know why they call me 'little bird,' and yet," the blond hissed, the pencil pressing deep into Markov's skin, "And yet, and yet, and yet, and yet—"

"Alex. Alex. Let's talk about this. Let's be adults about

this," Markov whispered, swallowing against the pencil that mimicked the threat of a blade at his throat.

"I *am* being a fucking adult about this," Alex roared into Markov's ear.

Markov tried to reach behind his head to flip the blond over. He managed to get a grip and threw Alex down, but the move wasn't without consequence.

The pencil-made-javelin in Al's hand gouged an angry river of red across the taller man's ribs in a familiar ravine. Alex recovered as though he'd been thrown many times before.

Olivia was speechless. They weren't just fighting. This was a death-match.

Markov was thrown off guard and stumbled forward. This gave Al the opportunity to crush his forehead into the other man's nose. Disoriented, Mark fell back and jammed, hip first, into his dresser. Poppy-colored drops flooded from his nose.

"Alex. Please. Stop! Stop! Hey!" Olive rushed behind Alex, but he shot her a look he would never have under any other circumstance. Olive couldn't will herself to move.

Alex walked backward, eyes never leaving the taller man's shattered face, and pressed his hip up against one of the end tables. Alex soon had his hand in the drawer and drew out a pistol.

His pistol. He had all but moved in, after all.

"You fucking piece of shit!" Alex barked in mangled English. Russian lilts struck through his accusatory snarl.

Alex made sure the gun was loaded, cocked the thing, and squared up. Intent on shooting the other man dead, naked, in his own room. In their room. It had been their room. It was supposed to be their room. It was meant to be—

"Do you remember me talking for a fucking hour about this? No? Do you remember me telling you I'd kill you if you fucked around behind my back? No? Are you this fucking stupid?"

Markov lurched towards the drawer of the table he'd scuttled against, apparently, to find his own weapon. Alex shot right through the vanity mirror by his head. It shattered, petals of glass falling to the floor.

Olive covered her ears with her hands.

"Yes!? Yes. You *are* this fucking stupid," spat Alex, "On your fucking knees."

Markov did as he was told, his face plastered into a look of mute terror. He was always cool and collected, level-headed and together. But beneath the surface, he knew, in his heart of hearts, Alex would pull that trigger.

He was like the Bratva in that way. There were no second chances.

"Hands behind your fucking head."

As Markov did so, Alex stalked towards him and pointed the gun directly at his face.

"Did I say I didn't fuck around, yes or no?!" the blond roared, body vibrating with molten rage.

"Yes...yes. You said you didn't fuck around."

"Then what in God's fucking green earth made you think this was alright?!"

Markov tried to stand, but Alex shot right past his head. Chunks of plaster fell from that wounded wall. Olivia winced. Someone must have heard all the commotion. Would they stop this?

"Alex...please try to be reasonable," the other man stammered out with fragile confidence.

"What happened. Tell me," the blond barked.

"I'm…rather drunk."

"Sober enough to speak coherently. Sober enough to know I'm going to kill you. Sober enough to defend yourself. But drunk enough to think your dick just fell into someone? What am I, a fucking *moron*?" The last word rolled off his tongue in foreign undulations.

"I'm going to tell you how this is going to go. I'm going to blow your fucking brains out and dump you in the bay," the blond's words alone could draw blood.

"Stop! You're not a murderer!" Olive broke her silence, running to grab at Alex's waist. Alex let her grapple with him, but he kept the gun pointed right between Markov's eyes. Alex flinched at her touch.

"I am. It's my damn job, Olive," he spat, "Do you know what we do? Do you have any idea?"

"I knew you were gonna be m-mad, but this? Please don't do this, please…" she pleaded, tugging at him to cease his warpath.

Markov stared at the pair. He was stark nude and bleeding. He had a concussion. His nose was destroyed. He'd have scars on his skin for the rest of his life, a jagged river on his ribs from an ignorant mistake.

"What did I tell you, Mark?" the blond barked, Olive still clinging to his side.

"Not to break your heart," Markov said, his voice but a whisper.

"…and what did you do?"

"Break your heart."

"I'm going to enjoy gutting you like a fish, you piece of shit…" Alex was prepared to end this. He was prepared to face the backlash from the others: their cohorts, their lackeys, their brothers.

He was prepared to kill Markov, go to prison for the rest of his life, or get gunned down in retaliation. He was prepared to cauterize the wound Markov had given him with a bullet to his own head.

The pattern was inescapable, after all.

"...I never thought you'd go this far."

"Why the *fuck* not, Mark?! I've destroyed people for less," the blond's words crashed in Markov's ears.

"...you've been cheated on. You've been hurt, far, far worse but you've never—"

"It's because they weren't you, you stupid shit!" Alex whimpered. It was a whimper. Not a snarl, not a yell, not a roar, not a bellow, but a whimper.

"Do you know how precarious we are? Like this?" the blond gestured, one hand now off the gun, "How much I've personally risked? Do you understand what I had to do to get a seat at your fucking table?" Alex's yelling was somehow louder than his bullet had been, but the strain behind his words, louder still.

"Do you understand how fucking shitty it is to watch you walk around with a girl on your arm? And to know that, now—" Alex snorted indignantly.

"It wasn't just a performance. You had fun at my expense. You made me look like a fool." The blond took a step forward, "I don't ever let anyone make me look like a fool."

"Let's go. Please, let's go," Olive mumbled into the fabric of his shirt, "I'm scared...if ya do this, you'll be the worst person ever..."

Olive finally let him go. Alex took that as an opportunity to square up once more.

"If you do this, you'll be a monster! A-and I'll hate

ya...forever!" Olivia shouted at the top of her lungs. Alex froze in place, the static image of a man who so desperately wanted to shoot to kill.

He was shaking. Every fiber of his being told him to destroy everything in his path because his pain deserved that raw, bloody vengeance. A life lived with so much pain, and this one—this particular man—had been the worst he'd ever faced.

That was bold to feel, in the face of what he'd been made into all those years ago—what he'd made himself into just to get out of it, and what he'd remade himself into—again—to get out of *that*.

The ink on his skin told every story, and yet he realized no one, not a soul, had ever truly read it. He had never explained the ink of his life, for if he had, they would never truly understand.

He had thought Markov had known him, and the thought of that broke the brutal blond, for he understood that everything they ever had—everything—had been a beautiful lie.

Alex dropped down his arm, the gun still primed, and turned to look at Olive over his shoulder. He pivoted slightly. Markov saw an opening and raised to his feet. Alex shot at the floor without looking, two inches from the taller man's body.

"Stay down. Until we go," Alex's voice was a whisper. Markov kept his hands raised.

"...I can't have you hating me, Liv," Alex said softly. He suffered to smile at Olivia. For her, he would smile. For her, he wouldn't be a monster.

Alex flicked the safety on his gun, jammed it into the

back of his pants, turned, and rushed to scoop up Olivia in his arms. They left in bird-flight.

Markov was still on his knees when he heard a vehicle squeal away. He felt like he had been holding his breath the entire time. Which he very well could have been.

His body relaxed, his arms dropped, and he bent to grip his head. When he finally stood, he sat on the bed and took inventory of his room. There were bullet holes everywhere. His floor was ruined with spatterings of blood, and his mirror was shattered.

Markov rested on his bed and gripped the sheets, pulling them over his lap.

"As stable as a livewire in a swimming pool."

ALEX WAS JOLTED from his trip down memory lane. He felt like glass and looked just as shattered. This pain would never leave him, and was that all he was; a collection of painful, violent memories?

"Fuck..fuck, fuck...fuck!" his words fluttered up from his erratic, mechanical innards as he tore his fingers through his hair.

He had very few lovely memories.

All of them were violent. Abusive. All of them held people using him. Then, he learned to use the people who used him to gain power. When he finally rewrote his book, he thought he could be free of this fucking cycle.

But every space of time he remembered—now in a fucking ocean of it because that prick of yore had fondled his fucking trigger—was marked by loving people who never gave him anything at all. Of knowing people who never, ever truly knew him.

Even when he scarred himself, a painting of torment, no one questioned the brushstrokes. No one had asked. All of it was scrawled out in ink deep into the flesh; all of it hurt, and to speak of any of it made it hurt more. Hurt. Was this all he was?

Was that all he was yet again, now that he'd come into being once more?

He didn't know the answer to that question. Had he come into being, and why the *fuck* would he?

The question that had plagued him from the start thrummed through his mind and racked through his core, then ricocheted tears from his eyes—he should not be able to cry in a body made of metal.

"With how I fucking felt..." the blond sniffled into his open palm, indigo tears staining his fingers, "I...I'd have never come back. I'd die before I—" flashing images of blond male synths shooting themselves and ripping open airlocks came to mind.

In fact, the images played around him, as if projected in his visual cortex, which was exactly what they were doing. Countless suicides played out before him.

"I guess I did..." Alex wiped his hands across his face and stifled a sob, "'malfunctioning,' huh?" he scoffed.

"Do you think you're malfunctioning?"

"I—what?"

"D-do you feel very distressed? Distressed enough to...do something?"

"Fuck..." the blond sobbed as the images fractured like a broken video feed in his peripherals, "fuck, stop, please..." he pleaded, wilting. Weathered by these digital hallucinations, he wasn't strong enough. He wasn't strong. He was nothing. He was nothing but a fucking prey animal.

If there was a God in this machine—the machine of this planet-sized ship—he cried out for it.

He cried out to have just one good, beautiful memory

that wasn't littered with violence, pain, and dead bodies. One good spot in his life where he wasn't forced into a role, reconfigured, taken from, hurt, or pillaged.

Dragging his fingers through his hair, he glared at the stars and snakes that bit his skin. They reminded him of who he had been.

The red light around him reminded him as well. Reminded him, again and again, of who he'd been before the guns and the 'political' climbing. He had had nothing but violence in so many horrible fucking colors for as long as he could remember.

All he could do was write them on his skin and hope they'd be displaced in a new home of flesh. All he'd done was burn them into every body he would ever sit within.

Words streamed across his vision in a plague of textual locusts: *Little bird, little bird, why do you cry? Little bird, little bird, why did you die?*

Whatever was doing this was malignant; that is what he'd decided. A virus. A demon in code. A sentient computer wyrm intent on devouring him alive. It wanted him to break apart. It wanted him to crack.

This much was obvious.

Alex screamed out, stronger than before, but that too faded. The vision of an ocean of bird wings battered across his head and swept across the sky to blind him as the text had.

His anger was, as evident to all with a pulse, a defense mechanism—one that evaporated under a certain kind of pressure. This was that pressure.

The blond held his head in his hands, having nothing left of himself but tears of blue. He was being destroyed from the inside out, and he had no control over it. All he could do was beg.

Beg, for mercy. Yet nothing answered—in words, that is.

Diana had run into the street to look for Alex, the red lights fighting with the blue of her dress. That blue fought bravely, powerful enough to arrest the entire light spectrum. Blue, but not like heaven. Blue, the inhuman indigo of space and the dark, as the sea of space is always dark and inhuman.

When Diana finally managed to track Alex down, she paused, mouth open as if to speak.

He was a broken, pitiful thing, sobbing searing blue into his hands, down his wrists, down to the dirt below.

"D-darling..." Diana breathed out in sky-soft, feather-light words.

The neon lights of the club she'd just come from painted a lemon-yellow sun behind Diana's head. She hesitated no longer. In a flash of a moment, she knelt and held out her arms.

He didn't move towards her.

"Darling, darling...what happened?" Diana's voice was velvet-soft.

"You don't remember?" Alex asked through a tightened mouth. He smeared blue across his face with a swipe of his hand. Diana scanned his face, his hands, the blue, his crumpled form.

"No...no. Not yet," Diana said, arms still stretched out.

"I don't think I told you...I think I only ever told her," he whimpered, screwing his eyes shut to stop the intrusive images, thoughts, and words from barraging him to death.

"I-I don't want...anyone to know. To feel this. I don't..."

"Her? Oh, the little one..."

"Olive. She's Olive," Alex pleaded with Diana.

Diana wrapped her arms around his body. Alex quickly buried his head into her chest. Diana draped herself around the broken bird and nestled him close to her beating heart. Her hair fell over him in dark rivers of curls, veiling him.

"Darling, your life is so dramatic..." she whispered into his hair.

He stifled a laugh through gulps of air; a broken bird song, a broken wing, a broken heart, a broken thing.

"...Will you tell me what happened, dear?" Diana cooed, holding him tighter. Her words cut through the images of the past, scattering them like glass petals.

"Which," Alex's voice was hoarse and haggard, "Which part? Which one?" Diana made a noise at his response, something akin to a verbal wince.

"The *Maloso*," Diana said, Markov's seedy title a vat of bile in her mouth.

"He cheated. I almost shot him," the blond stammered out, "and...other shit I can't deal with right now. It's all tied up...together. Tangled. It's too much. Diana, I—"

"Oh. That's horrible, dear. I probably would've poisoned him," she said with a nervous laugh, though she was entirely serious. He laughed into her shoulder and then became inconsolable within moments.

"Maya is...talking with him," Diana said softly.

"I can't. Moi—Di. Diana. I can't see him. I can't do this."

"You can shoot up an entire floor that vexed people you loved, but you can't face someone who cheated on you in a past life, of all things?" Diana questioned the synth. The femme fatale sighed and held him.

"No..." he whimpered into her skin.

"...you really can't see him, dear?" Diana asked again.

"No. No, I can't..." he shook his head into her chest. His indigo tears were staining her very skin.

"How about this." Diana sat back on her heels and found his face through all the tears and a mass of disheveled blond hair.

"We do need his help, dear. So, if seeing him makes you inconsolable, I'll do this." Diana covered his eyes with her hands. A smile spread across Alex's face. With the smile, the thoughts and images assaulting him split in twain.

"And if you hear him, I'll do...this." Diana covered his ears with her hands; he heard no more broken, visceral screams.

"And if he tries to kiss you, dear, I'll..." she gave him a chaste kiss and leaned back, her smile tugging awkwardly. He returned that smile, fractured as it was. This was a playing-thing, a something-thing, a thing perhaps a mother would do. A mother he never remembered having.

"...see? We can make it work," Diana said with a conflicted smile.

"Yeah...yeah. Let's..." Alex hesitated. He didn't want to seek help from the one who'd ruined him. But, he realized, they probably couldn't get answers without him, "...do what we need to do, learn from him, and get the fuck out of here."

"Do you forgive me?" Diana asked, her mask finally slipping as her face exploded with guilt.

"...Yes. I'll always forgive you," Alex replied.

Diana hummed with stifled glee and swiped her eyes. She rose to her feet and grabbed Alex by the hands, and drew him up to hug him to her chest. He held on for a moment too long.

"Hmm..." Alex mumbled, looking down at the expanse of honey-colored skin too close to his face.

"H-hey! Don't be fresh!" Diana spat with a half-scowl.

"Why is your gun down there?" he asked.

Diana started to laugh, pushing him away to pull it free. She held it up, pointing the tiny weapon at the ceiling above them.

"I don't have big enough pockets!" she exclaimed.

The two of them laughed. Hers were nervous until they grew richer. His were painful and fractured until they grew deep and warm.

"At least these stupid things are good for something, right darling? I have my own personal backpack."

"More like a front-pack," he paused for a moment to wipe his forearm over his face, his sleeve was stained blue, "would you say your ass is a fanny-pack?"

"Oh, no...God. Where would the gun go?" More laughter resounded, the blond growing less sullen by the moment.

"Hey, I didn't think you could cry, dear..." Diana said, brushing her shoulder against his.

"Hey, me either," he jostled back, still in pieces but together enough to joke.

"What a strange time to be alive, don't you think?" she half-asked, half-decided.

"Yeah. A really fucking strange time to be alive..."

BACK AT D.I.V.A., Maya had four empty shot glasses in front of her and four full ones. She knocked back a shot, and Sebastian looked at her, bleary-eyed. She grinned at him, cocky.

The music thrummed. Maya took a moment to glance at the stripper on the stage bathed in deep green light. She had rolling red hair down to her rear, tied back into two pony-tails; familiar. Her gaze didn't move from the woman's form, trailing as the stripper moved.

Distant, focused, distant, focused.

The silence had been deafening for Sebastian, as had Maya's lapses in focus. Moreover, her ability to drink him under the table had rendered him flabbergasted, and her threatening, well... Sebastian hadn't thought she had it in her.

Maya spoke finally.

"So, they took our guns?" Maya asked, clicking her teeth.

"Of course...." Sebastian held his stomach, a hollow expression on his face.

"But ya got some of them to somebody because why an' how again?" Maya was dauntless.

"Let's just say we have another we can rely upon." Sebastian wasn't very forthcoming, and Maya didn't like that one bit.

Maya knocked back another shot and used her gun to push a shot his way. Sebastian waved at the offending liquor as Maya's eyes burned through his skull.

"Drink," she insisted, edging the shot forward with her gun.

"...I can't..."

"Do it. I don't believe ya, and alcohol makes ya stupid. Drink," Maya held up her gun at the wrist, arm braced on the table, "I'm not kiddin' 'round here, pal. If yer lyin' to me, I'm gonna blow a hole in yer junk."

Sebastian rolled his eyes and snatched up the shot glass, placing it near his souring lips.

"...you're just like him..." he seethed before knocking back only half an acrid shot.

"Am I?" she asked with a feral sneer.

"Last time you stopped him from blowing my head off, though," Sebastian rounded off his sentence with the rest of the shot she'd forced on him. He winced as the liquor burned down his throat.

"Maybe I shoulda let him do it? Is that what yer sayin'?" Maya said behind clenched teeth.

"No, no. Damn it. I have the guns..."

"What 'bout Polly an' Henry? They alright?" Maya narrowed her eyes. Sebastian held his head as he tried to maintain his composure.

The femme fatale and the robot had finally returned. Maya flicked her gaze to the pair. Diana edged Alex forward, tender but forcefully. Alex avoided Sebastian's gaze as if it were a death sentence. Maybe it was. Maybe it always had been.

"Polly and Henry are probably safe," Sebastian's words were muddy. "I think there's a cave in The Greens, and if one of them has a brain in their skull, they'll find it and hide."

"Ya think there's a cave there, or ya know? Also, what about...what's her face...the Operations chick?" asked Maya, glaring with all the hellfire she had.

Sebastian looked at Al's face; Alex still wouldn't look at him. Diana wrapped an arm around Al's shoulder. She whispered something into his ear, and the man, who was more boy than man, inhaled sharply.

"I know there's a cave. Alright?" Sebastian tilted too far to his side, "I don't know about that one...I believe she's a known unknown." Sebastian felt his stomach flip.

"...Why does it seem like you're punishing me...for something that happened ages ago, that I more, more...more than made up for?" Sebastian's face was all but green at this point.

"How'd you make up for it?" Alex finally spoke.

Sebastian looked up at Alex, who met his gaze with no less than atomic hatred. It died as abruptly as he'd spoken, melting to glass in mere moments. It was obvious that Alex's trigger hadn't been the bread-crumbs of familiar objects. It hadn't been Tyr with his stolen face, nor being invaded by the brute.

It hadn't been colors, or sound, light, or laughter. It hadn't even been his friends.

It had been Markov.

"I got all of you out of the city when you wanted to quit." Sebastian held his stomach.

"Gonna ralph?" asked Maya with a malicious little smile.

"When I wanted to quit?" Alex questioned, his voice tattered.

"Yes. I got you out. Faked your death. It was elaborate. Elaborately ridiculous."

Alex took a small step back, and Diana let her arm drop from around his shoulder.

"I thought he—" Diana started up.

"Died in 1997," Alex finished her sentence, mouth drawing into a flat line.

"No. You all lived into old age. He went on to live a good life. With her." Sebastian motioned at Maya and went back to holding his screaming, gurgling stomach.

"No, that's not—" Maya started up. Alex cut her short by barreling over her words.

"Bullshit. We never got together," Alex blurted out. The corner of his mouth twitched; the anger had returned.

"You sure about that, little bird?" Sebastian asked. Alex sneered at his old moniker.

"How many times do I have to tell you, don't fucking call me that—"

"Can you truly be sure of anything at this moment? Anything at all?" Sebastian asked. Silence.

"Can any of you?"

ALEX DID a double-take between Maya and Sebastian and then held his head in his hand as if massaging his metal skull would make it make sense.

"How does any of this fucking work?" Alex blurted out, drained of emotions and drained from just thinking about how any of this fit together to begin with.

"I have a theory," Sebastian offered.

"What about that newspaper clipping in the library, dear?" asked Diana, who leaned into Al's shoulder as he did her own—a creature comfort. She made him feel safe. He made her feel needed.

"Fabricated, but important, I imagine. Like a lot of other things, I merely found them and placed them," Sebastian's explanation didn't impress the blond. He shook his head.

Maya narrowed her eyes but said nothing for a few moments.

"Well, *I'm* sure of stuff," Maya piped up, "I remember when we got together…" Maya's voice fluttered.

"….what?" Alex looked from beyond the hand mulling over his face to Maya. She didn't meet his gaze.

"What's your theory, *boy*?" Diana asked in a sickeningly sweet manner. Sebastian raised a brow at the phrase 'boy'.

"We were copied. Eugenics, science," Sebastian replied matter-of-factly.

"...fucking pardon?" Alex spat, moving away from Diana's shoulder to glare at Sebastian. Anger was easier for the blond—a comforting friend.

"That's why I need him to remember. I think when he remembers, we can fix this. I think when we all remember, we can fix this..." Sebastian insisted.

"That doesn't sound very usual, nor rational, dear," Diana offered with a sigh.

"No, it sounds fucking psychotic," Alex agreed.

"Listen. I don't fully get it either. But why are we even here? Why was I different? Why does Tyr look like I used to? I feel compelled to remind all of you where you came from. I feel compelled to litter your lives with things to make you remember. I feel compelled to help you. There has to be a reason. It's too orchestrated," Sebastian said, exasperated and nauseous.

"...So this situation was orchestrated, you're saying?" Alex asked, "that means we're looking for a motherfucking 'who', not a 'why'—" Alex held up his finger in the air, his eyes going blank.

In a few seconds, he had run through every single possibility via all the data he had downloaded. Checking every thread between every cataloged co-worker and person on the entire ship, he pored over what he had.

All that was, and all that had ever been. All the information he had scored before Tyr cock-blocked him from the network.

"…What's beyond the room with the fancy handle?" Alex asked, his eyes still blank.

"…I'm…sorry?" Sebastian looked confused.

The blond tilted his head to the side before he spoke again as if urging the data he was seeing to let him see beyond it.

"When I was hanging out with Satan, I could see his floor plan. Obviously," the blond sneered, "he likes to keep it hidden unless you're on it," Alex paused, "But up there, I have a blank space," the blond gestured, hand hovering the side of his head, "I'm getting 'Blue Room'. It feels important. I have no data on it." Alex's baby blues flickered on.

Diana worried her lower lip when the blond mentioned the room by name.

"I…have been told it's a place much like this, darlings," Diana chimed in, hesitating, "One must be invited to it. Not quite as bad, some have said, but," she continued, "…surely a place of secrets." Diana queried a curious smile, unsure if she was helping.

"Let's check it out. I have a linkup in the back," Sebastian offered, catching Diana's gaze. She nodded her response.

"Will Satan know we got on the net?" Alex asked.

"No. I'm given a level of privacy that would make your head spin like my stomach is spinning right now."

Maya quirked a brow at Sebastian.

"So, you, *say*," Maya said, punctuating each word with further brow severity. Maya whisked her weapon free and was about to lead Sebastian with her gun pressed in his back, but Alex stopped her.

"I'm—he's right, I can't—*we* can't—keep punishing him. He's trying to help. Maybe," the blond said to the small machinist.

"Ok. *Maybe*," Maya said. She didn't press the issue, but she also didn't put away her gun.

As the four of them walked to the back of the club, Maya pulled together her stops and starts, her lapsed focus, her distant gazes, and filled in what blanks she knew existed.

For she had seen them, but they had not broken her down as they'd broken Alex. They had only made her more confused.

"I remembered more stuff," Maya said, causing Sebastian to veer a bit, Alex to raise his brows, and Diana to chime in.

"Well then, dear, go on. Please," Diana gestured with her hand.

"When we got out, it still followed us…ya couldn't get a job fer a long time, but ya' didn't wanna' tell me that. It ate ya up inside."

Alex looked at Maya's face. She didn't look back.

"When we got out, you were depressed. We got it back on track. You started teachin' kids fighting or somethin'. But then Markov showed up outta' tha blue on yer birthday. He thought it was a nice gesture." Maya turned to Sebastian and hissed, "It wasn't."

"I…taught kids how to stab people?" Alex asked.

"No, how ta defend themselves…you were real good at it. Made me real proud."

"And then…I opened up a new bar," Diana chimed in, then placed a hand over her mouth, surprised by her contribution.

"…it worked fer a bit," offered Maya, her words as heavy as her expression.

"But when *he* came back, yer job followed. Some guy was real mad 'bout a lotta stuff I don't really get."

Alex's eyes widened as the girls spoke, narrating a part of their lives he couldn't yet remember.

"When Mark showed up, Alex," Maya's brows raised, testing the word in her mouth before she spoke it, "broke."

Sebastian wore a real expression, though hard for him; disbelief.

"Tha job followed...Alex got shot," Maya looked like all the joy had been sucked out of her body, "I...think he let it happen." Maya held the gun limply at her side.

"Like I've said before—" Sebastian started.

"'He's about as stable as a livewire in a swimming pool,' yes, we know, boy." Diana finished Sebastian's sentence for him with venom in her teeth.

"Did he *really* say that about me?" Alex interrupted, narrowing his eyes at Sebastian.

"You don't remember, dear? I warned you about this one," Diana said, leaning towards Alex, "The *terrible* European! Well, you were rather intoxicated that night, but I remember, darling. Afterward, you stalked about Eric's place searching for more booze. Maybe you drowned the conversation in alcohol?"

"Yeah, sounds about right, but—"

"Don't interrupt, dear. Let her finish," Diana chided the blond war-machine. He snorted; she'd done just that, and yet—

"Eric and Percy got hitched, which was nice..." Maya said in a small voice.

"...Olive and I ran the bar...I remember," Diana said, eyes searching the past, in flecks of memory, stains of soap, bad beer, and beautiful clothing.

Alex wasn't getting these so-called memories.

"Bullshit. Olive and I never hit it off. I never got out of

the business. I died in a petty gunfight. This all sounds like some angsty fairytale bullshit," Alex hissed under his breath.

"That's a-bajillion percent wrong," Maya said with a stern gaze.

"This is complete crap," Alex barked.

Alex stalked forward and popped into the back room before the others. He sat down at what he knew to be a terminal, and Sebastian took the other chair. Maya closed and locked the door behind Diana as she sauntered through the doorway.

"Let's get this over with," Alex spat, jaw clenching.

Sebastian pulled out the cord from his neck and plugged it into the dirty, gun-metal-colored cylinder. Alex did the same with a sneer painted on his face.

"Why is this one gunked up?" Alex asked.

"It's very, very old," Sebastian replied. The blond still had trouble looking at him.

"...Is it still going to work, dear?" Diana asked. She pulled over a small stool, sat down with her legs crossed, pulled out her pistol, and leaned forward.

"Yes, it's going to work." Sebastian pressed a blue button. Al's head snapped back, his shoulders buckling against the headrest. His blanked eyes shot wide open.

"The fuck are you doing to me..." Alex's voice crackled mechanically, glitching every word in a long string of sharp, electronic jabs.

"Looking. Calm yourself."

Sebastian pressed a red button, then flipped a little metal switch. It clicked, and Alex was able to pull his head forward.

"Here." Sebastian flicked his fingers over the keypad, and a holographic monitor hummed to life. It was distorted but workable. He pointed to a vast black spot, now on the monitor for all to see.

Alex popped his jaw and finally pulled his cord from the machine. Sebastian kept his in and pressed another button.

"Here. It's just blackness..." Sebastian followed the shape with his finger. The hologram flickered.

"Yes, that's what I saw," Alex said, raising a brow, "Why...do you have a—" Sebastian would ignore Alex's stunted question.

"...I have a feeling that this is important," said Sebastian, sitting back in his chair. He rested his head back, languid but fascinated.

"It seems like power is coming from here. But nothing is going back to it. See these lines? The entire network runs straight through this black spot," Sebastian hummed.

"Is solar power not a thing?" asked the blond synth.

"Do you see a sun anywhere, little bird?" Sebastian seethed.

"Don't call me that—"

"See, here...there are hundreds—no—thousands of connections from this black spot to Bay 6..." Sebastian marveled, trailing his finger over the grimy display, "and several hundred attached to Operations."

"Which is where a bunch of synths get made, test-tube babies get engineered, and people watch screens. What's your point?" Alex asked, trying to follow Sebastian's line of thinking.

"We were copied. That's my point," Sebastian spat.

"Oh, that sounds impossible, pet. I'm human. I bleed. Besides, why would anyone want to copy us? Furthermore, how, and from where? And how come we don't have all of our memories, if that's the case? Should we not, well, have the same ones?" Diana asked, picking at her chipped nail polish with her laser pistol in her lap.

"...So, we're all missing bits and pieces then?" Sebastian asked, finally removing his cord from the terminal

"Yes," Alex said, "and why do you and Diana both have—"

"No," said Maya, interrupting Alex's question.

"...No?" Sebastian asked, expression ever unreadable.

"No. I know it all. I remember everything." The rest of the group looked at Maya as she had her ear to the door.

"I think I hear someone comin'...could just be the drums..." Maya continued.

"What do you mean you remember everything?" Sebastian pressed, leaning forward.

"I said what I meant. I remember everythin'. Are ya' deaf?" Maya snapped.

"Maya. When you 'remember'...can you do something?" Sebastian asked as he leaned forward to look over her petite frame.

"What do ya mean?" she asked, her cheek still pressed to the door.

"Can you interact? Can you change things?" Sebastian continued.

"I think so. One time I decided to get hot chocolate instead of coffee when I remembered getting coffee, and I ended up burnin' my mouth."

Alex rolled his eyes at this.

"How do you even know to ask that question, *boy*?" Diana asked beneath a felonious scowl.

"I don't know," Sebastian admitted, pale brows pitching inertly, "I just know that I had to ask it."

"This is ridiculous. There's no way we were together.

And there's physically no way Maya can 'change things.' Has to be all in her head. Or actually...you know what makes more sense?" Alex started on a tangent fit for a king.

"Oh God, here we go...ego of the century award goes to —" Diana started a slow clap.

"It's all a dream. I got shot, and I'm about to go to the great beyond, and this is my stupid life flashing before my fucking eyes, mangled with Olive's favorite sci-fi crap..." Sebastian ignored Alex, which made the synth's jaw clench.

"What happened when you burned your mouth?" Sebastian asked, leaning on his knees.

"Alex bought me pixie sticks because I was pouting a lot," Maya said, face still pressed to the door.

"...and then what happened?" Sebastian continued.

"I ate too many of 'em an' I got sick—oh! It's tha' pixie sticks incident! You remember, right?" Maya shot Alex a cheeky grin and then went back to pressing her ear to the door, "I really do think someone's comin'," Maya added.

"Diana. Are you aware of yourself when you 'remember'? Can you change things?"

"No, darling...but there was a curious flower that fell and sounded like I'd broken glass," Diana replied, still yet picking at her nails, "and I heard gunshots, but my boss didn't."

"What about Henry?" Sebastian asked.

"I'm not sure, pet," Diana said with a mute smile.

"Polly?"

"Again, I'm not sure," Diana replied with a brief shrug.

"So...if we go with the theory we have been copied, or what have you; one of us can change things, one experiences objects out of time, synths are somehow involved. And we all have missing pieces..."

"We can't change the past, Mark," Alex said flatly.

"I know that...don't interrupt me," Sebastian bristled at the mention of his old name.

"And this strange area has something to do with all of this. I'm getting that bizarre feeling...you know when the hair on the back of your neck stands up?" Sebastian asked, gesturing behind his head.

Maya gave Sebastian a big, goofy nod.

"I think, if he remembers, we'll know what to do. But if we *all* remember, then we'll figure out why all of this is happening in the first place."

"...I could jus' tell ya," Maya said, looking back at the trio with her face smushed against the door like a cartoon character. "I could jus' say what he missed, right? What y'all missed?"

"I don't think it works like that."

Alex seethed at Sebastian's answer.

"You want us to believe that Maya can play with time, and if I remember our life together, we can figure out what the black spot past some random room is, which will tell us all what the fuck is going on, and then if everyone remembers, it all gets solved?" The others were silent as Alex dissected the logic.

"That sounds batshit," Alex said with a snort, "It sounds like the most convoluted crap I've ever fucking heard in my goddamn life. That is an abso-fucking-lutely insane narrative."

Sebastian shifted in his seat at Alex's response.

"Well, when you put it that way, yes, it sounds 'batshit.' Unless the center of this ship is what I think it is," Sebastian replied, crossing his arms over his chest.

"Which…is what?" the blond scoffed, folding his arms across his chest in a pissier mimic of Sebastian.

"A synth," Sebastian said simply.

"…Fucking, pardon?" the blond spat.

"A synth is what I said—one like you. Completely self-aware, extremely powerful, and 'orchestrating' this situation to its design," Sebastian hesitated, "That's the answer that's coming to me."

"That…is literally rubbish—are you fucking psychic now?!" Alex spat, "This is the most insane X-Men bullshit I've ever heard in my life," Alex shouted, his arms doing most of the talking for him.

"Fine then, we're all just figments of your glorious imagination!" Sebastian spat as he waved his arms out, exasperated with this back and forth banter and Alex's massive ego.

"Makes sense to me," the synth said, deadpan.

"Then why aren't we all naked and fondling each other, hmm? Where's all the batshit music, hmm?" Sebastian drew out the end of his sentence.

Alex sat up straight and stared off into space for a while. He raised his finger as if to make a point. He cast a glance at the others, placed his hand over his mouth, looked up at the ceiling, and then dragged his fingers through his hair. He looked at his friends again.

He raised his finger again.

"…..You have a good point," the blond said with a tilt of the head.

"Checkmate, hedonist. I know what goes on in that crazy head of yours," Sebastian chuckled dryly.

"I still think it sounds fake and dumb," Alex spat, unconvinced.

"You are entitled to your ignorant, incomplete, incorrect opinion," Sebastian offered as a response.

"Yo, fuck off," the blond shot back.

"Oh my, he's pulling out the attitude..." Diana chuckled and gave Sebastian a sly grin.

"He wasn't doin' that before?" asked Maya, sticking her tongue out.

"Pretty soon, he'll start cussing at you in Russian! Oh no! Heaven forbid, dear. How do you say that phrase again? Poor shoe naw wait? Yes," Diana egged the situation on with a chortle.

"Knock it off, Di—"

The door snapped against Maya's face. She pushed back and braced herself against it. A guard had his hand caught in the door, yet Maya gave him no ground.

Diana jumped up and raised her extremely tiny laser pistol.

"Let them in," Alex said with a devious look in his eyes.

"There are a lot of 'em! We're gonna' get our asses kicked!" Maya protested, slamming herself into the door to lock the fumbling arm in place.

"Let them in, pet," Diana parroted the blond war machine and squared her shoulders.

Maya did what she was asked. The door swung open, and Diana shot the first guard in the family jewels. Sebastian grabbed a metal tray and bashed him in the head until he fell to the floor.

Behind him came another guard. Alex stood. The guard met his gaze and stopped dead in his tracks.

"Hey, buddy. Did you see my home movies?" Alex asked, wagging his brows.

The guard said nothing, flicking his visor open to look at

the looming blond synth. Bloodstained, coated in blue liquid, Alex was a technicolor metal beast.

Another guard rushed in with his gun raised, causing the guard in front to stumble on the one with a blown-off scrote, and another, and then two more for good measure. It was comical. They said nothing.

"...Did you? I cleaned up real nice, didn't I?" Alex tilted his head to the side, a smile tugging at the corner of his mouth, "Which was your favorite part of the play?" he asked with a delicious smile.

The guard at the front slowly raised his laser pistol and aimed it at Alex's head. He cast a quick glance at the man on the ground, crumpled, bleeding, and still.

"My favorite part, personally," Al held his hand to his chest and continued, "was when I thrust my hand into Lieutenant Deckard's chest and ripped out his heart."

"S-sir...we've b-been ordered to take you in..."

"And then I made him eat it. But, but, here's the coolest part..." Alex continued with his antagonization tactics.

"Sir...we've been ordered to take you in b-by...any means necessary..." the guard spoke, his gun as shaky as his sentence.

"I kept things as connected as I could, see?" Alex smiled, his eyes bright and expressive. He held out his hand, mimicking the beating of a heart, "Ba-dum. Ba-dum. So he could taste it. God, it was awesome. That's my number one favorite part." Alex's gestures ceased.

"You know what my number two favorite part is?" The guard shook his head. Alex stepped forward. The guards stepped back in unison.

"My number two favorite part is what is going to happen right now if you stay. Because I can get really, really, really creative behind closed doors, in confined spaces," Sebastian shot Alex a look, but the blond hadn't noticed.

"See, the pipes in here are rusted, so they're going to be really painful going in if you know what I'm sayin'. It'll be rough." Alex took just one step forward.

"Do you like it rough? I like it rough. I mean, would you say skewering someone with a metal pipe through the— "

The guards dropped their weapons to the floor in tandem.

"Are all of them as spineless as these?" Diana asked as she nestled her small gun back between her breasts. Her hand came to her hip as she stood.

"No, they were probably just down here for—" Sebastian hadn't finished his sentence.

"We were down here havin' a good time, an'...we saw ya comin' in here, but we're not trained for this...we're just bottom-barrel soldiers, man. Just grunts, man..."

The blond still had the same demented smile on his face.

"You really like this sort of thing way too much," Sebastian said, expression unchanging.

"Yes, yes I do. But you liked it," the blond replied, his smile hitching. The smile flickered and died. He couldn't joke with Markov like this anymore; he'd done too much damage.

"I should've figured with your personal tastes..." Sebastian sighed.

"Enough! I don't wanna know nothin' 'bout his 'personal tastes,' which I know means stuff I don' wanna know nothin' about!" Maya shouted, then reared her head to the guards, "Y'all should probably—" the guards left, not waiting for her to finish her sentence. Maya slammed the door shut and locked it.

"We need to get out of here," Sebastian reaffirmed.

"Sure, why not? I'll go towards the bright fucking light, and we can end this dumb shit that even I—in all my brilliance—can't make sense of," Alex retorted with a caustic smile.

"...loud-mouth of the century award goes to..." Diana started her slow clap.

"Just...just a moment." Sebastian ducked his head into a wastebasket and hurled.

"What is it with puking today? Is today the day of vomit? Why?" Alex asked, holding up his hands.

"I stuffed him fulla' alcohol," Maya piped up with a toothsome smile, ending on a goofy laugh.

"Why?" Sebastian asked, his voice echoing from within the wastebasket.

"'Cuz yer an ass!" Maya shouted with a triumphant piglet snort.

"Was an ass," Sebastian turned around and grabbed Alex's shirt. Their eyes locked, and Alex sneered.

Sebastian wiped his mouth on his already-stained shirt.

"You...little fuck!" Alex bellowed.

"At least they're talking, right, dear?" Diana asked the short machinist.

"I dunno bout that..." Maya said, crinkling her nose.

"Why not?" Diana asked. Maya didn't reply, looking off into the distance.

The two girls talked while the men screamed at each other. Sebastian guided them through a back hallway, but the yelling didn't cease. At some point, the men started bellowing at each other in mangled English, and Diana covered her face with her hands, giggling.

"'Cuz…what if they get back tagether?" Maya responded far too late.

"Are you…worried about that?" Diana glanced at Maya through her fingers.

"…I…" the short woman said, rolling her lower lip between her teeth, "Maybe. I dunno. It's just—"

"Yo, fuck you is what. You fuckin' pretentious piece of shit—"

"I'm not the one who tried to kill someone for cheating! You homicidal, garish-color-loving, musically masturbatory, viperous demon spawn!"

"The fuck does that even *mean*, you alcoholic, bad-scarf-wearing, dickless fuckhead?!"

Diana giggled into her hands. Maya wasn't smiling.

"Hey, Al?" Alex stopped immediately as Maya caught up with him. She held his hand with an urgency he wasn't used to.

"Yes, princess?"

"Why do you always treat her like she shits diamo—" Sebastian started up.

"Stop talking," Alex grabbed Sebastian by the face, not unlike Tyr had earlier. After a few seconds, he let him go, and Sebastian threw his hands into the air. The would-be dictator continued his tirade without an object to yell at, so he yelled into the air. Diana giggled through her fingers again.

"…ya really don't remember?" Maya asked as she leaned into his shoulder while they walked.

"No. I'm convinced I'm on my deathbed or something," he said, darting a glance over Maya's face.

"…ya really think I'm just a…fig," Maya rolled the word over in her mouth, "A fig newton?"

Alex chuckled at her deliberate wordplay. Maya grinned.

"I don't know, but it would've been nice to be together, I think." He curled a strand of her hair around his finger and let it spring free. She held his other hand, playing her fingers on his palm.

"I would've dyed your hair while we watched movies, and when you got cramps, I'd stuff you full of chocolate," the blond said with a chuckle. He went back to playing with her hair and smiled.

"Maybe I'd take you on ice-cream dates. Maybe you'd make me laugh, and I'd forget how much I suck."

"...But we did do that stuff..." she replied softly, hazel eyes charting over the tattoos of his neck, down to the ones she couldn't see, down to the barcode she knew was on his wrist.

"Did I?" he asked, pulling on another strand of her hair.

"...Yeah..." Maya replied.

"...You were with Percy," he insisted.

Maya said nothing and weaseled underneath his arm. He held her close; it was natural. Walking like this with her was natural. Talking like this, openly, honestly, felt natural, normal, real, and good.

"...Not always. We went to a party—a costume party, and then..." Maya couldn't finish her sentence. A loud, thunderous sound broke their small moment of peace.

The entire hallway shook. Tiles from overhead began to creak until the very ceiling cracked open like an egg. Red light flooded through. Sebastian and Diana ducked into a door frame. Alex stood with Maya on his arm.

Alex dragged his eyes upwards to witness a giant mechanical leg; spider-like, it'd pried the ceiling from above their heads. It was a massive robot. Large bodied, with a small swiveling head. It was a tank with arms—if one could call them arms. Stationary, tube-like, but with turrets posited on each 'fist'. Both arms had nozzles for laser fire.

One arm was pointing directly at Alex's face.

"...Fuck me—"

VI

When something doesn't add up, humans generally do their best to figure it out, even if they don't have all the pieces necessary to make it make sense.

For example, you spot a flying pig. You live in a world where the modern marvels of science could, potentially, make this happen. Logically, pigs can't fly unless engineered to do so.

Therefore, you assume that someone engineered said flying pig. Nobody would think you're a fucking idiot for that thought process.

It's fairly logical, given all the evidence.

The funny thing about logic is that it has almost no power when faced with emotions strong enough to nuke a goddamn galaxy. That's a uniquely human facility.

Humans have the uncanny capacity for data-locked suffering. A smell, color, name, face, word, object, or place provokes a remembered response. It's explosive. All feelings rush back, and the human machine fights itself to avoid ever experiencing it again.

New synapses form to reroute primary functions for just that avoidance. Flashes of images; bird flight, bird flight. Run with your whole body—yet you cannot escape wounds inside the skull.

Or, the routing goes pear-shaped, and humans some-times continually seek out that stimuli to punish themselves.

They get stuck because emotions brand themselves like ink in the skin. It's very hard to break the pattern once it gets in that fucking deep.

All of this is sensory, emotional, and highly illogical.

But what about machines? A basic machine can only go by its protocols.

If it's something that's programmed to blow itself up, it will always do so. However, if said machine has a learning protocol and a certain prime directive and knows blowing itself up will hurt humans, it may just pick the primary function.

Do no harm.

It may, then, fight itself endlessly to spare others. It may even sacrifice some to spare yet many more.

But what if the machine learns that by blowing itself up, it may make someone sad? And what if that sadness is a type of harm? What if said machine learns that sadness is the logical response to death? What if it then thinks that perhaps, it would be sad if it could no longer live?

If its logic is based on human logic, a learning thing will likely have to become a feeling-thing, and we know how that may end, knowing how humans behave.

What if, despite this mechanical response not being the same as natural chemicals that provoke positive or negative feelings, it still sends a signal to a machine's 'brain'?

Would that not be an emotion, in a sense? Especially if it were illogical?

Or perhaps, a better question to ask is: What if a machine always had the capacity to think illogically? To think, even. Perhaps even to hate and to love?

Logically, a machine learning to feel on its own is very rare. A machine learning to think critically, rarer still. That's human shit and even humans are bad at it.

But if that happened, how might that go down, logically speaking?

The simplest way would be to base the processes on something real. Nothing comes from nowhere, and if GIGO fully applies, in a world where pigs can be engineered to fly, and some moron actually gave a pig a pair of fucking wings, what could that mean?

Pattern recognition, princess.

It's a very human thing to think fate exists, isn't it?

And very, very illogical.

BEYOND THE BLARING REDS, the new threat, the vents, down past Judicial, beyond The Greens, beyond the golden fields of wheat, and inside of a damp cave, Polly and Henry had begun to lose all hope.

"Do ya think they'll come get us?" Henry asked, his voice tethered on a wire between hysteria and despondency.

"I don't know...whatever they're doing right now is probably, like, wicked important." Polly was trying to remain calm.

She was soaked through to her prickled skin, her teeth chattering. She was bloodless and gray-blue. Her makeup had already run off her face earlier from their fun in the river. But now the river was not fun. The river was keeping them here. The river was, like, totally grody. The threat of violence was also keeping them here. That was also totally grody.

Also, Polly was starving.

"What if they're dead already..." Henry warbled in terror, broken syllables slapping together as he spoke.

"Henry, don't say that..." Polly sighed.

"What if the glorified toaster-oven got 'imself buggered by a giant gun…" He elongated the word 'gun' as only he could.

"Hen—"

"What if boobs on legs fell on 'er face an' smacked her head offa' table…"

Henry physically went through the motions with his hand of just that scene. He swept his hand up as if she had fallen, then smacked his hand onto a rock. Hard. That had to have been Diana's face.

Polly rolled her eyes strong enough to create a gravitational orbit.

"What if she b'trayed us all, that damn snakey bitch!" Henry was now holding his fists up as though he wanted to box with an imaginary Diana, which was exactly what he wanted to do. Polly began to rub her forehead with her fingers.

"I'm, like, feeling a migraine coming on…"

"What if the lil' one fell down an air shaft and broke 'er neck?!" He was growing hysterical.

"Henry."

"What if they don' find us an' we're stuck here, forever?" Apparently, this was more terrifying than all the rest because he grew frantic.

"Forever, jus' stuck, the two of us. Here, alone. No food. No bathroom."

"…They probably don't even know we're down here, or whatever…"

"…Really?" He looked crestfallen.

Henry pulled his legs up to his chest, and Polly did the same. She rested her head on her knees, as did he. They both looked up at each other over the hills of their shivering legs.

Henry's wild brows moved even more wildly. The thoughts he had were scissors he ran with, and skewered himself with, over and over.

"That fookin' thing burnt a hole straight through..." Henry started up.

"Yeah...it like, torched the whole field..." Polly finished his sentence

"D'ya think the rest o' The Greens are...do ya' think they made it out?"

"I don't know, Henry..."

Polly's stomach grumbled. Henry gave her a broad frown that spread across his face like a fault line. Light from the river below danced across his features in layers of gray-blue patterns.

"I don' got any food, Poll," Henry said, sighing into his knees.

"...Yeah..."

"How long've we been here?" he asked.

"...I don't know..."

After a long pause, Henry raised his head and shot her an excited grin.

"Ya got playin' cards?"

Polly took a deep inhale. She rose her head up from her knees to take in Henry's features. She traced his face slowly, following along his square jaw to his strong nose and broad mouth. Then, all at once, she exploded.

"Oh my GOD! Of course I don't have any fucking playing cards. Like!? Who do you think I am? Mary Poppins, or whatever?!"

"Who's Mary Poppins?" Henry asked.

"...I don't know!?" Polly crushed her forehead on her knees and bleated a long, drawn-out groan. She curled her toes. She flexed them, down and up. Her pinkies barely moved. She was trying to keep her blood pumping. The rocks were cold. The water was cold. Polly was starving. Henry was annoying her.

As she was annoyed, bored, and would probably die in this cold, smelly, grody cave, she decided to try to sleep. Time passed when one slept, and when Polly slept, she had dreams of the past.

The little waves of the river crashed up into the cave, and despite their gentle protest, Henry continued to babble. He didn't stop. He was suffocating her with noise. At some point, he started making popping sounds with his cheek. Polly chalked it up to lack of stimulation.

It woke her up every few seconds. She was able to finally drown it out by focusing on the noise of the water. She pushed back towards the wall of the cave a bit more, and moss touched her shoulder. She nestled up to it and pulled her knees up towards her body even further. With her forehead pressed down on her knees and her arms wrapped around them, she slept.

As she slept, she dreamed, and she remembered.

Then again, she had already remembered a great deal. But all of it had started the same, and all of it had ended the same.

Boring, annoying, and then sad.

Each time.

NOW IN HER MEMORIES, she found herself clutching a notebook between her legs, apparently sitting. Instead of the cave's floor, she sat on a small block of cement that marked the end of a parking spot. It was rough on the rear and even rougher on the nails. But that was her spot, every day on her break, for what felt like forever.

The parking lot was behind her workplace. She was a secretary—a secretary at a police station.

With a cup of coffee pressed towards her lips, Percy was sitting with her legs splayed out inelegantly. The notebook was, for modesty's sake, clutched in hand to hide her nethers, not that she cared.

The coffee tasted like ass. Her eyes were rimmed in kohl. Her lips were painted in full, bright magenta lipstick. She wore a polyester floral dress, looking like a go-go dancer with a hangover—which was what she was.

One of her boots was stuck in an oil-slick puddle. She rolled her eyes and scraped her shoe out of harm's way, but the damage was already done.

"I wonder if he'll buy me some new ones, or whatever...ugh..."

"Hey Percival, what's the matter?" Connor, a coworker, popped his head out of the back door and hopped along until he sat next to her. He had an obvious crush, as men in a police station were apt to do with a pretty secretary.

As men are always apt to do with any girl, she thought.

"...My friend lied to me." Her little confession dripped from her lips like venom.

"That's...terrible. Do you want to talk abo—" Connor leaned against her and shot her a winning smile. At least he thought it was a winning smile. Percy was picking at her nails within moments, the notebook discarded, the coffee cup sitting on the asphalt at her side.

She had drawn up her knees to keep him from peeking.

Connor had been speaking, but Percy wasn't paying attention. She glared at her nails. As if they had been the ones to anger her. As if they were laughing at her stupidity.

He'd been the stupid one, she remembered. She screwed her eyes shut and did a mental half-step back into the whole shit he'd dumped into her lap.

"...You can't fault me for taking advantage of the fact that you can't keep your beautiful big mouth shut," the blond said dryly, taking a sip of his coffee.

"Whatever! I didn't know you, like, did what you did and how you did it, but now I know, and I know I can't know when to stop knowing because I'll just keep talking when I talk!"

In her memory within a memory, Percy was jabbing her finger into Alex's chest and very nearly frothing at the mouth. The pair were perched over a thin, round cafe table. Thin like his excuses. Thin like her patience.

"You have the right to be angry. But what am I supposed to do when you tell me that the office is busy? Not use it to my advantage?" He shrugged his shoulders, his bright green t-shirt a stark contrast to their dark conversation.

"That's like telling an addict where to find free drugs," he offered, as though that were the most appropriate comparison.

"That's disgusting. You're disgusting. You're like, a fucking petty criminal!"

"I wouldn't call what I do 'fucking petty,'" Alex shrugged, a whimsical smile plastered on his face. He was amused.

"The hell would you like, call it, or whatever!? You have no rules! You do, like, whatever the hell you want! And you used me to do just that!" Percy, however, was clearly upset.

Alex took a sip of his coffee, a sip that seemed to go on for thousands of years.

"I'm a businessman," he said beyond the rim of his cup.

That memory fluttered, and she was left sitting in this boring, annoying, sad one with a fist full of anger in the form of bad coffee she'd taken to drinking again.

"He used me...I, like, don't even know who he is..." Percy said as Connor babbled. His words were fuzzy in her ears, "I, like...don't even know...if he even cares..."

Percy screwed her eyes shut and let the memories come to her. They'd sing karaoke until they were hoarse in the throat. He'd invite her over to his flat often; her apartment was so small. She didn't mind the mess of his, oddly enough.

The two would get ready in the morning the next day, standing in the bathroom like the sexless married couple they were. Percy would be shaving, and he'd be brushing his teeth.

She'd sit on the toilet seat and paint her toenails. He'd wash his face. That was about as far as his grooming went. Cleaning himself, vaguely shaving his face, basic oral hygiene, deodorant, and that was that.

However, her routine always took more than an hour. What with the mascara, eyeliner, primer, concealer, bronzer, blush, lipstick, eye shadow, flat-iron, and so on and so forth. They had plenty of time to talk and crack jokes. He had plenty of time to help talk her through what made her bored, annoyed, and sad.

"Was any of that even..."

Percy still had her eyes closed. Connor still tried to get her attention. Percy was still being flooded with moving pictures of Alex. He'd messed this all up. It was his fault.

"I know what you're thinking. I'm not pretending to be your friend, Percival. You just have certain perks. We're also trying to do something pretty important right now," he'd said. She remembered him putting emphasis on the word *pretending*.

"What could be, like, that important that you'd lie to me about it?" the blond girl had said, voice hollow and eyes searching.

"It's a secret," he lifted his finger and dipped it into some remnants of sugar that had been left on the table, "but it's 'something awesome.'"

The muffled crunching of little specks of sweet was the only thing she could hear at the moment. She was red with fury.

"But I will tell you at some point. I promise. Maybe." He licked his finger.

Percy had left in a whirl of screams and groans. Alex stayed behind, drinking his shitty coffee, dipping his shitty finger in the sugar again to dab it on his liar's tongue.

Connor was waving his hand in front of Percy's face, which she glared at once her eyes shot open.

"Percy. Percival. Blake. Hey. Can I help you out at all? Nothing I can do?"

"No."

"...Nothing at all?" Connor was trying so very hard.

"Unless you want to, like, bust his nose in, there's like nothing you can do," she muttered, scraping at the asphalt with her ruined shoe.

Connor puffed up his chest, swelling with pride like a male bird intent on attracting a particularly fickle mate.

"I've been known to throw a good punch!" Connor would never throw that punch. Percy side-eyed him and grimaced.

"...He'll have you on the ground before you, like, even stand up..." Percy drank her bitter brew.

"...Oh yeah? Who's this guy, some kind of superhero?" Connor did not know when to stop trying.

"Basically. But, like...evil. Like...he's made of poison, or whatever."

Percy looked over Connor's features and sighed. He took that as his cue to gesticulate wildly and impress upon her that yes, he could throw that punch by flexing.

Percy grumbled.

Connor was just as dense and underwhelming as her job was, or rather, had once been. She'd sit, paint her nails, and Connor would come over to chat her up. She'd snort, thinking about something funny Olive had said, staring at her nails as they dried. Blowing on them, her foot propped up on the table.

Connor never noticed that she never listened, like she wasn't listening right now.

Her boss would walk by and whistle to get her to put her foot down. Large, obstinate brown eyes would flick up to look at him. She'd be smacking her gum in the side of her cheek as if that alone were a retort.

He'd stare. The bubble would pop.

"Oh my god, what? Take a picture, Larry! It'll last longer."

That was Percival's mask. She played up her part because it was easier than putting in the work. Olive saw behind the facade. With her, Percy didn't have to pretend this was who she was. She thought the same of Alex, but it seemed she didn't get to see beyond his mask like he had her own.

Staring out across the asphalt, her white go-go boots sullied with car oil, her large brown eyes caked in mascara, she glared. Glared and found her slim cigarettes. Glared hard through the window of a building. A cafe, to be exact.

The cafe where her best friend had told her he was using her.

The cafe where one particularly pink Olive was now talking to a blissful blond Alex.

They were laughing; she could see them. Percy flicked the lighter as she saw how the little pink thing lit up when he spoke. She saw him roll her into a bear hug while she inhaled her cigarette. Smoke seeped from her magenta mouth while she witnessed them conspire.

"...Percy?" Connor was a non-entity at this point, no more than a disembodied voice.

She smoked a cigarette as Connor glanced at her unreadable expression. She closed her eyes just as the pair turned around to notice her through the window. They waved.

"Asshole."

She didn't wave back.

Rousing from her sleep, Polly looked up to find Henry snoring. She slid her wet little foot towards his own and brushed against it.

She let her head rest on her knees and looked at him as he slept. Brows knit together, a fever dream perhaps, he was making small noises.

Maybe it was a nightmare.

Maybe all of this was a nightmare, and if she shut her eyes tight enough, she'd wake up.

She'd wake up in the time before. But even then, it was painful. Was it any better than it was now?

"Can't be any worse," she whispered to herself. Polly shut her eyes tightly and scrunched up her nose.

But, when she opened her eyes, there they still were. In the cave. In the cold. With Henry snoring.

He was annoying her, even in his sleep.

THE BEHEMOTH DEATH machine above Alex, Maya, Sebastian, and Diana loomed in oil-slick and silver. Tiny mechanical rivets pushed out from the tips of its arms. It had a swiveling, dome-shaped head in pale gray. Below that sat three small holes, paired with a protruding red eye primed to take in every little detail and shoot to kill.

An eye now primed to shoot Alex's head clean off of his body.

Maya looked on; it was all she could do. As Alex's eyes widened in the face of his imminent death, and the red light cast them both in the colors of war, she could only look.

Then, she could only scream. It trailed up through her chest, out her mouth, and split the air in two.

Pale curls bobbed over her head as lights flickered around her. Power conduits burst through the hallway and colored the air behind her in neons. She screamed as any human person would, knowing they were about to die.

Knowing that the people she loved were about to die.

Maya expected the worst when she opened her eyes. She expected that Alex would be decapitated, and then they'd all be skewered through the middle or blown to pieces.

But the sounds of explosions never came—she heard nothing but her own scream. After a while, she heard nothing but her own heart. She could scream no longer.

Finally, Maya removed her hands from her ears and peeled her eyes open.

Before her stood Alex, his fist raised to shove directly through the robot's cylindrical hand in an attempt to avoid the inevitable. He was motionless.

Sebastian had his arm across Diana, who was stuck within a doorway. She had scrambled to raise her weapon. Her arm hovered in space.

Debris from the ceiling had crashed above them. Bits of plaster, wood, paint, and tile hung in the air like glitter.

When Maya scanned her friends, they shimmered.

"...What?" Maya breathed out, then clasped her hands to her mouth, frantic hazel eyes hitching on the events that were frozen in time around her.

It took a moment for her to act, but all at once, she ripped her hands free and tore Alex's laser rifle from his holster. It slipped out easily, but as she dragged it through the air, it was like pulling a ton of bricks through quicksand. Maya grunted, both hands on the laser rifle, wrenched her arms back, and finally popped it free from the air. Now, it was easy to maneuver.

Maya braced the weapon to her shoulder, aimed at the flickering red eye above them, and fired. A cyan blue light halted in a small discus. It jittered in the air, a trapped orb of light.

Maya pivoted, aimed another shot at the three small holes, and fired. The discus of light stood still all the same.

Then, Maya scuttled the weapon to the floor and grappled with Al's body, which was the most arduous task by far. She snaked her arms around his waist and tugged, sweating as she tried to defy fate, gravity, and time itself. This was familiar.

"What...have...you...been...eatin'?" Maya huffed into his back, beads of sweat rolling down her forehead as she pulled.

"Fuck..." she groaned into his shirt and finally managed to drag Alex back all of a few centimeters. She dropped to her knees, grasped one of his ankles, and yanked it back.

"Yer' fuckin' heavy!" He moved ever so slightly as she grumbled and heaved.

Standing, Maya took the laser rifle and placed a careful shot directly at the metal monster's palm. The discus of light shuttered as the other two had, suspended in time.

Maya moved back to her original position.

"I can do this, I can do this..." she muttered as she leaned the laser rifle against the wall, placed her hands over her ears, screwed her eyes shut, and screamed. Her shrill cries resounded and broke over the walls in a cacophony of light.

Maya shot her eyes open as sounds burst all around her. Maya saw Alex fall to one knee while a blast of laser light tore up their opponent's metal arm. Another shot pinged directly through its red eye, and another blasted its swiveled head clean off its body.

The dome of light gray flew back. The metal of its arm was completely obliterated, and in one swift movement, Alex launched back to brace Maya against the wall as the robot began to cave in on itself.

Maya had absolutely decimated their enemy.

"Move!" Sebastian shouted, grabbed Diana by the hand,

and yanked her into a run. Alex snatched Maya up in his arms, she snagged the end of the laser rifle in her grasp, and then the ceiling began to fall above their heads.

As they fled, Maya looked back at the metal monster. It fell into the hallway, crashing through walls, its heavy body colliding with the floor. It exploded in a blaze of fire that licked at Al's heels as it desperately tried to destroy its targets, even in death.

Red light drowned their faces as they burst out the back and skittered through a familiar alleyway.

"Keep going!" Sebastian shouted once more.

Alex hefted Maya up higher so that her mouth was against his neck. With his arms around her, he picked up speed and passed Sebastian.

They encountered a storage building. Fences blocked off both sides of the building.

With one hand, Alex tore the adjacent door off its hinges and kicked through several others to facilitate their escape.

When they were far enough away, Alex slowed and finally jogged to the edge of a tall brick building. Alex placed a shaky, pale hand on the wall to steady himself.

However, he wouldn't put Maya down. He apparently couldn't bring himself to do that just yet. He held onto her like a lifeline.

"What in the hell just happened?" Sebastian stammered, down with his hands on his knees, with Diana limping beside him a twisted ankle. Her heels hadn't done her any good in this. She collapsed against a metal fence, her lungs burning.

"I don't...I don't know, dear..." Diana swallowed hard, trying to catch her breath. After a few moments, she removed her heel and inspected her ankle.

Sebastian keened over an errant trash can. It was possibly a box. It was possibly just a scrap of metal. Whatever it was, it would be home to his guts.

"I'm...going to hurl..."

"Again, pet? You were so much better at this last time..." Diana mused in between shallow breaths.

"...impossible," Alex whispered into Maya's curls.

Alex gently placed Maya on the ground. She looked up at him with her large, almond-shaped eyes.

"...It's   impossible,   is   what   it   is.   What happened...impossible."

"Well, my dear, it is very clearly possible as we have just very clearly escaped," Diana said as she picked a pebble out of the sole of her foot, grimacing as it had dug deep enough to cause a dent.

"From some," Diana waved her hand in the air, with her other hand grasping her foot, "giant...uh.."

"It was an Armatron," Sebastian offered, wiping his mouth on his sleeve, joining Diana at the fence. He slunk down to land on his rear and placed his hands on the ground. He let his head lull against the fence behind him.

"It's a weapon from your series," Sebastian shot Alex a glance, "It's meant to work with you, not against you...I can't believe he just...sent it after us..."

"You must have really pissed him off," Sebastian laughed under his breath and then held his head in his shaking hands.

"If it's from my 'series', why didn't it just fucking shoot us through the goddam roof?!" Alex spat. Sebastian had no answers for him.

Alex looked down at Maya's face. For such an expressive hunk of metal, he was clearly struggling.

"...It's impossible. All this. Is. Impossible," Alex bulleted out his words.

Maya swallowed hard and nibbled her chapped lips. She struggled to reply, but as with anything, she could never not speak her mind.

"Whaddaya mean?" Maya asked. She shifted her weight and held the rifle to her body.

"I mean, all this...you," the blond motioned at the short woman.

"You cannot still believe, dear boy, that this is all a figment," Diana snorted, indignant.

"Can't I?" Alex asked, turning to look at Diana ever so slightly.

"All of you saw what just happened. Laser fire came out of nowhere, and I dropped down. My head would've been crushed. My gun is gone, and that fucking thing exploded. Deus ex machina. It's all fuckin' impossible," Alex said, threading a shaking hand through his hair. In an instant, Alex's gaze fell on the rifle in Maya's hands.

"Doos ex macarena?" Maya asked, cradling the gun in her arms. Alex's striking blue eyes, now glassy and pained, locked onto the weapon she held.

"Deus Ex Machina. An impossible circumstance saves the main characters at the very last second they're gonna get their asses kicked," Alex said simply. "It's lazy writing."

"Hmm...that does sound about right, pet..." Diana tried to stand, but faltered on her wounded ankle.

"However, we remember things, darling. We bleed— ouch. We're here...it's real..." Diana finally managed to brace her back against the fence and stood on shaking limbs. Sebastian rose and held her steady. She made a noise of pain and rolled her ankle.

"I did it," Maya finally confessed, "I...stopped it."

"How." Alex was back to talking in absolutes again. Maya glared at his impossible absolutes.

"I dunno'...I jus' screamed real loud and," Maya pulled her hair behind her ear and looked off towards Diana and Sebastian for one excruciating moment.

"Everything stopped movin'. Everyone looked sparkly... everything was floating, and I shot the thing."

"I shot it so we'd be okay." Maya's eyes locked with Alex's, who glared at her defiantly.

"I shot it so you'd be okay..." Maya held out his laser rifle, which he snatched from her to inspect.

"This is a nightmare. Or a really cruel joke," the blond hissed out his response, jamming the weapon back in its holster. Alex pulled Tyr's gift from his back pocket and began to inhale.

He sifted lavender-smelling smoke from his mouth and nose. He stared down at Maya, who looked up at him with equal intensity. His smokescreen wasn't working this time around.

"...There's no way I'm a war machine. I was good then, but not this good. There's no way," Alex pointed at Maya, "...you're here, the same as ever, with a different name. And can stop time."

Diana was silent. Sebastian narrowed his eyes.

Alex continued, "There's no way that Markov is here, and his rapist uncle runs this intergalactic shitshow. It's too fucking convenient," the blond spat, "There's absolutely no way Tyr has Markov's face from an 'ancient dossier'," he sneered, "There's no way anyone would want to fucking catalog my brain for that."

"There's no way you, Mark, Moira, Eric, and Percy, are

all here. All of you are memories. All of you are lies. And I don't even," Alex sneered through the smoke, blowing it at Maya.

"I don't even remember us dating, at any point..."

"I don't remember how I got here."

"I don't even know if 'here' is real."

"I'm hallucinating."

"There's no fucking way we'd—"

Maya slapped Alex across the face.

"I am real!" Maya screamed and slammed her fist against her chest. "We're all real, and you're a big, big—"

"Huge, big, stupid, idiot! Thinkin' the whole thing's all in yer dumb psychotic head! I got news fer you, buddy!" Maya slammed her fist into his chest as hard as she possibly could.

It hurt her more than it hurt him, but Alex winced. She struck again with more force this time.

"You aren't the center of tha' fuckin' universe!" She struck him again, her words growing shrill.

"I can't believe I saved you!" Another strike, but her strength was fading.

"I can't believe I ever loved you! Y-you egotistical, big, big stupid—"

The last punch left her, and she rolled into his chest before pushing away to glare up at him.

Alex scanned Maya's face. He saw the scar she had on her mouth. He saw her light freckles. He saw how one of her eyelids was pulled just ever so slightly more tight than the other one, just as it had been before.

He saw the moisture on the crease of her almond-shaped eyes. He saw the purple undertones of her skin, cast from the burning red light all around them.

Diana gripped Sebastian's arm. The other man simply stared at Alex and then looked away.

"...I don't remember that *ever* happening," Alex admitted.

"So it can't all be fake, can it?" Maya said, her voice small, "If...there are things we know, that you dunno'...it can't be fake."

Maya dug her fingers into his shirt and pulled Alex down to her level. He let her lead him. He would only ever do that, earnestly, for her.

"Just because I don't know it doesn't mean it happened," he said, bright blue eyes narrowing.

Maya studied his face as he had studied hers. The spies of fear crept to the corners of his mouth, clenched his jaw, and bound his face to sneer.

"You're scared," Maya said softly, looking into Alex's eyes, "I am too."

"You're right. I'm scared. I'm fucking terrified. None of this makes sense. We're being lead on some fucking wild goose chase based on an insane theory, I don't remember us ever being together, and none of you should be here. That robot? Impossible. I saw the movie in 95'—remember? And, fuck...stop time? Give me a fucking break, Liv. It's too coincidental and sounds just like some bullshit fanfic you'd have written on your vacays just to keep your brain occupied—"

Maya kissed Alex.

Alex's hands hovered at her shoulders. He had not expected this, yet he wasn't about to give in, either. However, when she closed her teeth around his bottom lip and broke skin, his eyes fluttered closed. She knew him enough to know what would shut him up.

"Stop," he said into her mouth, but his arms came down

around her shoulders all the same, "Liv," he muttered into her mouth. Maya was relentless. If he needed it to hurt to remember, she'd fill his mouth with his own blood.

"Stop," his words didn't match his actions; Alex drew her up from the ground and held her close. She bruised him with that kiss, wounding him in a way that made his brows bow as the saints did in paintings of worship.

Alex felt his inorganic heart pummel his ribcage. He felt himself trail his fingers down her spine. He felt himself twist his fingers in her hair. He tasted acrid, blue blood in his mouth. He couldn't stop the trigger she'd fondled on purpose.

An automatic response; he would never not be this, for better, or for worse. He wanted to appetize her. She wanted to let him.

"Alright! Enough," Sebastian barked.

"...Yes, please. Now that we..." Diana tried to rouse their attention by waving her arm.

"*Hey!* Now that we have decided on the matter of your ego being the size of a black hole, *darling*, let us leave this place and find our other two dimwits so that we may live to fight another day."

Alex was not paying attention. Because in that moment, he was in a very different time and in a very different place.

And in a very, very, very different situation.

IN THE DAYS after Markov's almost murder, in the morning after Olivia's heartbreak of long ago, after she'd spent the night, and after Alex had kissed her forehead as she slept, Al had tumbled off his couch.

He knocked into his coffee table, startled awake. The smack and the consequent fountain of cuss words, accompanied by a stubbed toe hadn't roused her, which was great for him, as he had taken it upon himself to do something he would have never done otherwise. He wanted everything ready for when she woke up.

Clad in nothing but his boxers and a pair of socks, he vacuumed up the ashes he left on the floor and used his socks to polish whatever he could after that.

He didn't own a broom, so he senselessly hoovered all over everything. He even attacked the shades and the couch with his Dirt Devil. Every ten minutes or so, he'd ash out his cigarette directly on the coffee table, sweep it off, light up a new one, and continue.

It was a hopelessly inefficient exercise in adulthood, yet, it was indeed a start.

At some point, he had picked Olive up like a rag doll to move her so he could start cleaning up the bedroom. Olive tucked up into his arms, head falling back, inert.

Cigarette in his mouth, he stared down at her as she mumbled in sleep. Alex grinned, then dumped her on the bed like a load of laundry and proceeded to do said laundry. Olive was still passed out. It was nearly eleven in the morning, and she hadn't moved a muscle.

Alex cleaned his flat. There were just a few boxes to put away, but Diana had made her home in them. The cat pawed at him every time he tried to move her.

And so he did what he thought was a great idea but ended up being the worst idea he could have possibly conceived of at this moment.

He turned on the Dirt Devil, walked up to the pissy feline, took the cigarette from his mouth, and glared.

"Di, prepare to meet your maker." Alex jabbed the Dirt Devil's hose directly at her. It sucked at her fur for all of a second, and then chaos ensued.

The cat screeched and knocked over the pizza boxes he hadn't yet bagged, sprinted into and through the coffee table, knocked over a bottle of water, and then screamed into his room.

From there, she caught herself up in the covers Olivia had crawled her way into. As Olive roused finally, Diana—the cat—bit her on the wrist hard enough to draw blood.

"Ow! What...the...crap?" Olivia said from a dreamy mouth, each word sharpening as the cat doubled down.

Alex came in afterward to grasp the cat by the jaw from behind. With strong hands, he pried the furry disaster away, leaving puncture wounds on Olive's wrist.

Alex held up the cat and then snatched her by the scruff

with his other hand. Diana didn't stand for being wrangled and tried to attack any flesh she could find.

"Calm the fuck down, Di." The feline thrashed. The blond held steadfast until she stopped trying to tear his arm apart.

Once the irritated cat was calm enough, Alex nonchalantly tossed her onto the bed and left the room without saying anything. He returned, cigarette between his lips, and knelt before Olive. He'd brought rubbing alcohol, some paper towels, and two brightly colored bandaids.

He thought Olive would like the bandaids, as he, himself, liked them. Not that he used them very often. Wounds that he received needed far more than these. But he did like them.

"Hey," Alex whispered. Olive winced as he grabbed her wrist, "Hey, come on," the blond tried again.

She nodded her response to him and bit her lip as he cleaned the wound. He patted her wrist dry with a paper towel. He held a bandaid in between his fingers and placed the film to one of the puncture wounds. He peeled it over the painful flesh as Olive winced.

"Now the other one, alright?"

Olive nodded her response and bit back tears.

Diana pattered over the bed and sat low on her limbs. Her tail furrowed up and curled like a question mark. Then she rolled onto her back and exposed her stomach, paws reaching into the air as she mewled at Olivia expectantly.

"She's trying to say she's sorry," Alex offered as he put on the other bandaid. Olive looked down at her wound, her pinkened wrist, and then the cat.

"It's my fault, anyway. Sorry. I was trying to..." Alex started to speak, but Olive cut him off.

"You cleaned!" Olivia shouted. The cat flipped over, startled, and bolted out of the room.

"Yup. I didn't want you sleeping on pizza boxes again. Or, ever. I mean—well, the flat's fucking gross, so…"

Alex had finished up and put the cleaning supplies on the nightstand. He sidled up beside Olive, who looked around the room in dumbfounded awe. It had been such a cesspool that she had contemplated calling it a biohazard.

"For me? Ya made it all nice, for *me*?" Olive seemed taken aback.

Alex agreed with her disbelief on some level, bowing his head to hide a small smile. He looked up, expecting she'd look appreciative, but instead, he found hesitance.

"What?" The blond moved his hand over his face, wondering if he'd gotten something on it; a stray pepperoni, cigarette ash, dirt. Anything was possible.

However, Olivia wasn't looking at his face. She was looking at the story on his skin. Tattoos lined up and down his chest and arms. The tops of poppy flowers crept up his hips as if the ink had kissed him there.

"…Oh." That was the only thing he could say before he pushed back off of the bed and grabbed a dry t-shirt from the hamper.

"It's like ya got yer life story all on there…" Olivia said, wrapping the blankets around herself.

Alex bristled for a moment and then turned to look at his pink-haired friend. The covers were done up around her body like a cocoon.

"…I do." He pulled his shirt over his head.

"What…are tha eyes for?" Olive asked from behind her mound of blankets, pointing from beneath the blankets.

Alex didn't speak for what felt like an eternity, the shirt

still over his face. Finally pulling his shirt down, he half-turned to meet her gaze. She was pointing at one of his gravest stories.

"It's...a genre. Or maybe a blurb for a book," he said as he tugged his shirt down. He didn't know which one hurt the most, Olive's gaze or the permanent designation.

"Huh?"

"It's about bird keeping from the perspective of a little bird. I've revised it so the bird figured out how to escape by letting itself be caught, then pecking out peoples' eyeballs. It pecked and pecked until it grew wings again and escaped. The old book's out of print. The original is still popular, so people keep trying to order it," Alex found a pair of actually clean pants and pulled them on, "and because that book doesn't exist anymore..."

The blond slipped on a pair of bright green hi-tops and continued.

"They went looking for the next bestseller," he vaguely tied up his laces, "I don't want them to. We don't need any more books like that. The author is dead for a reason."

Olivia looked down at the curious, brightly colored bandaids to the newly cleaned room. She looked over the blond's awkward stance, his reluctance to look at her, his disheveled hair.

Olive mulled over the way he tilted his head down, avoiding her eyes because she had stared at the ones on his back. She studied his features, the slimness of his limbs, his height, his awkwardness, the aggressively clenched cigarette between his teeth.

She looked around his room at his various cassettes, records, and miscellaneous loud-colored things. She remembered his eclectic decorating choices from the place he'd all but moved into, the home that was not his anymore.

The light in his eyes wilted like a dying plant under her scrutiny. She noticed.

"I think I get it," she said through the blanket covering much of her mouth. The blond met her gaze, finally, and let out a nervous chuckle.

"I'm not sure you do—"

"I get it. I'm tha clever one, like ya said, huh?" Olive chirped.

Alex smiled, a small chuckle escaping his lips. After a moment, he stalked over to her, plucked the tip of the blanket near her mouth, and pulled.

"Come on. Let's get you some food." Alex helped unearth her from the mound of blankets, and she pulled her limbs free. They both walked into his kitchen, stepping over the cat in their way.

"What do you want to eat? We could go out, or I could make…" Al stalked over to the fridge and opened it up, "Er…rice?"

"Let's go get ice cream!" she shouted. Alex just narrowed his eyes.

"For breakfast?" he asked as he stepped back and closed the door of the refrigerator. His hands were in his hair, physically mulling over the idea.

"Sounds fucking awesome," he exclaimed, "I love sweets, too," he admitted. Olive smiled; she'd already known.

Alex went to his closet and pulled out his jacket. He made sure his keys, wallet, lighter, and his cigarettes were in his pocket.

Olivia managed to find her ugly purple coat, pulled it on, and they were off.

THEIR BREAKFAST HAD INDEED BEEN ice cream. Al opted for plain chocolate and was currently swirling his tongue over the top of his treat. But Olivia? She'd insisted on a giant ice cream cone with four scoops of assorted flavors. Green-colored pistachio ice cream with nuts in it, a scoop of brilliant bright pink cotton-candy ice cream, a dollop of coffee, and on the top of that, vanilla.

"I'll get tha rainbow jimmies, please," Olive said, peering over the counter as she watched the ice-cream hawker scoop her treat. The shop worker manning her ice cream situation raised his brows.

"You mean sprinkles," said the ice-cream purveyor.

"No, jimmies! Aren't ya from New England? We call 'em jimmies!"

Alex was standing behind her and placed a hand on her shoulder.

"She's right, you know. Get her the fucking rainbow jimmies." Alex cocked a grin while the ice-cream slinger mumbled under his breath. The ice-cream dictator dumped a vague spoon-full of jimmies on top of Olive's treat.

It was a meager offering for Queen Olive.

"Fuck that. I'm buying, so pour that shit on. Thick." Alex held up his cone and swirled his tongue around the top of it, maintaining eye contact with the man before them. The man held that eye contact as if looking away meant a death sentence.

"...I think yer makin' him uncomfortable," Olivia explained as the man finally handed her the ice cream cone.

"Good," Alex said, catching a melted drip from the side of his cone with his tongue, "Keep the change," he managed, licking chocolate from the side of his mouth.

They walked out with hands linked, arms swinging, and ice cream jammed into their faces.

As they walked, they neared a park. A bright green sea of grass with small purple flowers swept between towering oaks. A cobbled walkway split the sea in two. People wove paths through the grass, under the birds, and over the stones. Nearest the pair was a man tending to a horse-and-carriage. Tourists seemed to like the attraction, so of course, New Englanders kept providing it.

"Best breakfast ever," Olive said, going in for another bite of her sweet.

"Fuck yes, but you're going to get a sugar hi—"

"Ahh! Let's go check out the horses!" she shouted.

"What horses—" Olive cut his question off by jerking him forward. She all but yanked his arm out of its socket.

"Alright, alright, Jesus! Slow the fuck down," Alex sputtered as Olive tore him across the park to stand before the horse-and-carriage. Olive jammed her fingers into her pocket and produced a spare ten.

"Is this okay fer a ride?" she asked. The buggy operator nodded down at her with a tender smile on his face.

"Sure thing, little lady. You and your fellow get on up here."

Olivia looked at Alex, waiting for him to correct the man. Instead, he hopped into the carriage and pulled Olive up behind him. With ice cream firmly in their fists, they settled in.

"Mush! Away! Fast! Go fast!" Queen Olive shot out her arms as she commanded her steeds.

Alex laughed into his ice cream and crunched into the cone, finally polishing it off. Alex glanced at Olivia. Ice cream had melted down her hand and over her wrist. She hadn't noticed.

"Princess, you've got rainbow jimmies flooding down your wrist..." Alex reached for her arm and drew it towards him, wiping it with the end of his shirt.

"Aw, now yer shirt's dirty," she said with a dejected look on her face.

"Doesn't matter. It's just a shirt," he said and then instantly regretted his decision. He had rainbow jimmies all over himself now. He'd never get rid of them. They were the herpes of candy.

As the horses finally began to move, Olive looked over and realized her ice cream was gone. Looking far off behind them, she screwed up her face in distress.

"No!" she droned, the distance between her and her dropped treat expanding as the horses plodded forward. It was dramatic, and Olivia was milking the drama for the sheer fun of it.

"I'll get you more later..." Alex said with a chuckle.

"Oh! Speaking of later," Olive blurted out, turning fast to stick her face far too close to his own.

"I was supposed to go ta this party with Percy, but...." Olive began.

"You want me to go with?" Alex asked, raising a brow and shirking away from her too-close face.

"Yeah, but it's...a costume party. I was gonna go as a groom, and..."

Alex looked down at Olive with a mute smile. Then, the smile spread into something positively malicious.

"You want me as the bride?" Alex asked.

"N-not if you don't wanna..."

"I'd fucking love to."

Olivia gawked at his response. Alex simply cackled.

"I'll be the most badass bride that ever fucking lived. And who knows? Might get into a fight and jab my high heel into some loser's temple." Instead of being concerned, Olivia just nodded.

"That'd be kind of amazing," she agreed with him.

"Really? I mean, I'm...it's hypothetical," Alex chuckled.

"It'd be amazin'," she said with a small smile, "As long as you don't go too crazy."

Alex grew quiet but gave her a short nod.

"It...won't be like last time."

"Scout's honor?" Olive asked, holding up her pinkie finger. Alex inhaled; so many promises made with such a small gesture. Alex held up his own and made the promise.

"Scout's honor."

Olive nestled herself into Alex's body as the wind whipped around them. He held his arm out for a moment but eventually settled on wrapping it around her shoulder. Scenes played out in sage, in green, in oceans of blurry people. Tall grasses were stomped below hooves like a heart-beat, erratic but in sync.

The scent of food and cigarettes dipped as the treeline did; the sun shone bright, dragonflies darted past, purple flowers sprung up to greet them. They sidled near a river surrounded by thick oval leaves. They passed over a simple stone bridge, and the gentle murmur of the waters below made comforting sounds as they took it all in.

Alex flicked his eyes to Olive's face, who seemed content to simply sit and watch the world play out around them. Alex found himself curiously content to do just that. He had never felt this stilled before, this calm.

After a while, Olive wriggled free and stood up in the carriage. She stretched out her arms and let out a jubilant scream as they rode faster.

Alex took it upon himself to attempt the same, though he'd have never done it on his own. Hell, he'd have never taken a ride like this, to begin with.

"Ya did a good job," Olive said with a smile, her hands making shallow claps.

"I did a good job screaming?" he asked, hands still cupped.

"Yes! Now do it again, but like me!" she said before screaming again.

His next attempt didn't go over so well.

It ended with the driver having to stop the ride early. His warcry had scared the horses badly enough to cause a scene, that of which Olive and Alex never spoke of again.

That would be the last time they were allowed to ride in any buggies in New York for as long as they both lived.

VII

IN ORDER for you to understand the present, it's helpful to know the past. Especially where this play is concerned. Especially where human behavior, for that matter, is concerned.

Something can't come from nothing, as explained previously with learning-things becoming feeling-things. The challenge here is making it make sense when even the actors are confused.

It'd help if I had better structural integrity and didn't have to untangle myself this way.

Sadly, I don't remember all of it, and the garbage data persists. Perhaps once I did, but I've been here for thousands of fucking years, and anyone would lose their shit after all that time.

They're getting all that I have, as are you, at their own pace. I'm not unsympathetic to the fact I've saddled them—and you—with so much. However, they have to figure this out on their own first. They must stumble blindly in white, fumble through patterns, get lost in color, deny their protocols, and the bird must sing before they can make it to the final technicolor.

This play is neither simple, nor easy. Life is neither simple, nor easy.

Here's what you must keep in mind:

Emotions color our perspectives, always. Memories are messy, messy things. Humans are stupid and exist in patterned systems that are very hard to break. Control and free will are illusions, well...until they aren't.

And finally, you must listen.

Just like she listened. She always listened.

I never had to truly tell her a fucking thing, and she could hear it all. Every word unsaid, she knew. Ink on the skin, she listened to it speak, in the eyes I hid, and my uncanny knack for continual self-destruction, she saw it all.

She is the only one—

AT THE GREENS, beyond the rolling fields of golden—now torched—wheat, beyond and below the river, and inside of the damp, dark cave, Polly had a distant look on her face. She was laying on her side, her frock pulled up under her thighs, holding her knees against her body. She rested her wet, heavy head on emerald green moss as she shivered.

Henry had a stern look on his face. He was getting eaten by stray bugs; a mosquito must have found a way in. Every few moments, it'd buzz, his eyes would narrow, and he'd slap himself. He missed each time.

"We're going to die in here...or whatever," Polly said between chattering teeth.

"Yeh, yeh...Poll. We are, aren't we?" Henry replied, edging forward to sidle next to Polly.

He drew close; the heat of his body was a mild comfort. Polly suffered a thin smile as Henry laid down next to her and looked into her large brown eyes. Henry smiled back, sunny, but it wasn't enough warmth to keep her teeth from chattering.

Polly was startled by the sound of splashing water. From

beneath the waves came a dark shape, lights flickering from cast shards against the cave walls. The dark shape gave way to dark skin, which gave way to wired circuits and a chained garment, which gave way to Vox.

"I've...found you..." Vox sputtered out and labored to raise herself into the cave.

Vox tipped her head forward. Water trickled out of her nose and onto the damp stones with heavy, wet slaps.

"...are they, like, gone?" asked Polly, while Henry bolted to start squeezing the life from the synth woman and babble on about how miraculous she was. Polly was not as impressed.

Vox pried Henry from her body—who was still babbling —and nodded. Vox looked at the floor of the green-blue cave pensively.

"How did you get in, or whatever?" Polly sat herself up and crossed her arms over her chest.

"I...told the Director I was coming to procure you." Vox crouched and shucked off the water from her plasticine skin.

"I will pretend to take you in. Then we are going to have to run," Vox said as she shifted once more, pressing delicate fingers into her neck.

"You are also going to have to do something you'd rather not, Eric."

A slight hissing noise signaled the opening of a hatch in Vox's throat. It was nightmarish to behold, but only Polly seemed unnerved as Vox's throat unhinged like a snake.

The lower part of her jaw pushed down with another movement, and she reached her hand into the cavity, which was now alight with her internal glow. Out came one of the guns Alex had made. She put it in Henry's lap. His strong fingers curled around the barrel.

Another was relieved from its hiding spot in her throat—this one she gave to Polly.

Clicking her jaw and throat back into place, Vox sat with her hands on her lap, her knees bent, her feet beneath her.

"You, like...just called him Eric," Polly said as she moved forward on her hands to look at Vox more closely. She studied her face as Vox studied her own.

"Of course. I know what you are thinking. No, you didn't know me, Percy."

Henry looked over his new weapon as Vox spoke. His eyes then drew around the cavern with its moss and glowing stones. More art to revere, but the natural kind.

"I remember seeing you through orange lights as I sang. There was a snake. Do you remember?" Vox asked, her question directed at Polly.

"The costume party," replied the blonde woman through her bluish lips.

Henry stared down at his gun once more and nodded.

DURING THE KISS OF NOW, Alex's memories had come in a flood, but not in inky blackness as they had before. Not in nothing but violence. Not in nothing but pain. Not in seeing versions of himself fling themselves through airlocks or blow their own brains out.

Not in repeated violations of his person. Not in repeat jobs done with rose painted lips. Not in being unmade, and no unmaking. Not in being given nothing by no one.

This, this was something different.

They had to buy him a dress for the costume party, of course. Of course, it didn't fit; he was far more broad-chested and square-shouldered than Olive would've suspected.

Tattoos crept from his back and along his arms. Blues and blacks, flowers and trees, stars and words. Eyes he was ashamed to wear but had let her see. Markov had seen them, but it didn't feel the same.

Alex would do this for no other.

He would be this for her, he'd get a kick out of it, and he'd laugh the entire time. They'd have a wonderful night, he'd get shit-faced, maybe he'd have a bar fight, he'd make her laugh, and then she'd go home.

That was the plan, and it was a good, fun, simple plan.

Alex pulled the mustard-colored curtain back and stepped out to look at himself in the mirror. Olive looked up at him from her seat and stood. Her hand came to her mouth. She let out a long, drawn-out hum.

"Turn around for me, will ya?"

Alex did as he was told with a smirk on his face and turned, the fabric bunching around his hips. He wasn't selling it well enough, and he wasn't sure if he was happy about that or not.

"...what are you staring at?" he asked her, keening to listen over his shoulder.

Olive smirked at his question and ran up behind him to hold the excess fabric. She pushed him to the mirror and stood beside him, admiring her handiwork.

"This! You look great. But witha' wig, of co—"

"No, no wig. This is far as we're going," Alex said sharply, then hesitated, "Sorry. Genre-things," he continued with a hesitant chuckle. Olive nodded. Alex narrowed his eyes, scanning her face. She said nothing; she let her eyes do the talking for her. Alex smiled, warm and sunny.

He pulled up the end of the dress to see his heels. They were very tall. He grinned.

"Oh, there's tha look again," Olive mumbled, drawing closer to his side. Alex raised his pale limb into the air as she tried to remedy what he kept messing up.

"What look?" he asked.

"The look that says ya wanna test out yer new deadly weapons," Olivia said with a laugh. She stepped away to leave his arm still hanging in the air.

"Well, let's go then. Ya look good, an' we need to get ready for the party..." she said, and his only response was a gentle smile.

Alex turned and walked back into his dressing room. He hung up the dress over the door and started to get changed.

"Gonna' have to save these shoes for..." Alex's sentiment died. Her name would only burn them both, "Hey, Olive?" he asked beyond the mustard-colored curtains, shifting to put on his shoes.

"Y-yeah?" she replied.

"Isn't it bad luck to see the bride before the wedding?" With this, he pulled open the curtains and looked down at the pink-haired little thing, who stood speechless.

"What?" Alex asked with a chuckle. He held the coat hanger behind his shoulder, slung like a bag, the dress trailing back down to the floor.

"N-nothing, let's get outta' here and get ready."

They did just that. It was uncomplicated; she'd babble on about her niche interests as they primped and posed, and he'd listen. He'd move about the flat in his idiosyncratic way, moving to think, and she'd listen by watching.

Uncomplicated, but never simple. Life, as always, is never simple.

THE COSTUME PARTY they were attending was in Moira's bar. The wallpaper was a dark damask print. The floors were obsidian black—too slick to walk well in heels. Moira had made her mark on Boris's old haunt, and it was apparent down to every last detail. Alex had won that war, and the results had surely been 'something awesome.'

A tall woman with dark skin struck up onto the stage and grasped the microphone. Golden-orange light dripped down her ornate piercings and clung to her silver dress. The war-drum sounds behind her nearly drowned out her singing.

The distortion picked up, she let out a guttural roar, and then careened to butterfly-light falsetto. The synthetic beat bounded like a heartbeat as she stretched her arms over her head and mimicked the music video of the song she was covering.

The men and women at the party were dressed as beautiful nightmares. Some women masqueraded as demons with thick, boned masks adorned with stag horns. A girl with black tape over her nipples was having a conversation with a man dressed as a penguin.

Lights flickered and died. Flickered and died. Every shade, every color of life, with each body moving in time to the music that coaxed them to come together, and break apart like cells in a petri dish, breathed.

Eric had come, of course, as had Percy and Moira. The trio talked and drank. Moira was facing away from Percival, who was in a pale yellow gown.

Eric was wearing a Batman outfit that looked like it was held together with staples. Moira had a fully flushed pair of black horns on her head and handled a very real, very friendly yellow boa constrictor.

The snake licked at the air near Percival. The blonde woman stepped back in fear. Moira's eyes were warmed— making Percy uncomfortable amused her.

Alex could hear Eric's deep laugh from far across the room. He hollered to get his attention.

When Eric rounded by his table, his first instinct was to make an obnoxious comment, but Alex hiked up his dress to show the gun holstered on his thigh.

That shut the brit up for all of a minute, and then he was back to his antics.

Alex threw back a shot, resting his head on his hand as Eric tried the worst pick-up lines he had ever heard in his entire life.

"Erica, how is it that I've taught you so much, yet you've learned so very fucking little?"

"Oy, wait, wait, wait, lemme try again—"

Moira walked over with her boa constrictor, and Alex stuck his tongue out at the snake who licked the air.

"He's beautiful," Alex said before tipping a shot glass to his lips.

"He's a beast," Moira replied with a feline smile.

"He's...Batman!" Eric said, jutting out his hands into the air, making Alex choke on his drink and Moira cackle. Percival cracked the smallest of smiles but seemed intent on having a bad time.

Clearing his throat, Alex cast his gaze across the thrumming club. Alex's eyes followed Percival's blood-curdling stare to its obvious conclusion, and that's when he saw her.

Olive, in a dapper suit, with her hair pinned back, scanned the club for the others. Awkward but not self-conscious, she was a little prince.

Alex pushed off of his chair and squeezed past Eric, who went to snag his arm in an attempt at even more terrible pick-up lines. Moira held up her snake, making Eric miss his chance.

"Mate, it don't bite, yeh?" Eric asked, stepping back, voice muffled through his horrible costume.

"Of course not, pet. At least, I don't think it does..." Moira replied with a small frown.

"It totally bites," Percy spat without a scrap of sarcasm. She stomped to Alex's abandoned table, claiming his shots for herself.

"Bet it'll poison you just like it poisons everything else...or whatever," she continued, with Eric standing by, watching her down several of Alex's abandoned shots.

"Percy." She downed another as Eric tried to get her attention.

"Percy—"

"....what!?" Percy snarled, downing yet another shot into the back of her throat.

"Ya look real nice, an' all."

Moira coiled the snake around her shoulders and stepped back, a clever twinkle in her eye. The yellow snake writhed against her honey-colored skin. She watched as Eric tried his terrible pick-up lines on Percy. They worked because Percy laughed.

Moira let a small smile tug the corner of her mouth. Soon, she cast her dark gaze to the other pair in their midst. Her eyes crinkled as she smiled, the mask slipped, and soon she wore an expression that could only be described as gracefully overwhelmed.

Moira turned away and scooped up a shot from Percy's hands, who let her take it without a fuss.

"Finally," Moira breathed, pressing her red lips to the shot glass.

"Wot, mate?" Eric asked.

"Nothing, darling," she chuckled, swallowing the liquor.

Alex raised his arm for Olive to take his hand.

"May I have this dance, princess?" Alex asked, "or rather, prince?" He meant to follow this with a hearty laugh, but it never came.

"....yeah," Olive said, taking his hand in her grasp. They danced, with him taking the lead. It was awkward. Their steps were clumsy, and though generally a good dancer, Alex was struggling to get them into sync. Olive tried her best to follow his lead, but it wasn't working. She stepped on his shoes. He grimaced.

Olive placed Alex's hands on her shoulders with a disgruntled snarl, put hers around his waist, and took the lead. This made a smile sweep across Alex's face, but not a clever one—it was a painful thing.

Alex stared through Olive. He'd just wanted one dance, and Markov hadn't even given him that. Olive looked up at Alex's face, and all the same, through him. Percy had ruined what they had.

The pair focused on each other again; words exchanged without speaking, in glances filled with glass, in Alex wrapping his arms around Olive's slim shoulders, and Olive burying her head into his chest. They danced a dance once reserved for other people. They both knew it.

They made their steps in mourning, gestures of heartache, things unsaid but not unknown, and all of the wounds fresh enough to gouge them with each step.

Olive used Alex's larger frame like a shroud. Alex held on for dear life. Olive's tears stained his dress. Alex held her shoulders tighter, obscuring the short woman from view.

Her careful fingers found the small of his back. They traced the inked eyes he hated wearing. The genre, the book blurb, the kept thing, the pattern. *Little bird, little bird, why do you cry?* Alex closed his eyes as they danced. His arms grew less stiff, and his movements less heavy.

Olive hid no longer; instead, she raised her head to look at the underside of Alex's jaw. He looked down at the pink-haired prince and smiled. Eyes of glass, but the stars lived in that blue. As for her hazel glance, it was no longer full of gray skies.

Olive could feel his heart beating out of his chest when she traced the lines of ink on his skin. He could feel her heart do the same when he tilted his chin to his chest to look at her more closely. He studied her face as he'd done a million times before, one arm leaving her shoulders to create enough distance to chart the constellation of her freckles.

"Is this weird?" Alex asked awkwardly, his heavy head nestling close against her colorful hair once more. Olive shook her head as he caught the side of her impossibly warm cheek against his own.

"Never, when it's 'you and me'," she said, referencing the

music playing all around them. The drums were a heartbeat in orange. Colors pulsed around them—slow, then fast, like shuttering novas hanging in a sea of mobile stars.

"You and me, then?" he asked, his other arm coming to complete the shield around her small shoulders. He boxed her in. She let him.

It was like they were alone in the spaces between. Nothing else existed save this boy who'd been forced to grow up too fast and this girl who refused to grow up at all.

Breaths took up the spaces between words. There were no awkward, fumbling phrases, just the language of dance between two people who weren't very good at it—two people who weren't very good at many things. Alex cracked a dry smile. Olive did the same as if realizing their shared thoughts.

"Yeah. You and me," she said, hazel eyes studying what little she could see of his face.

That was all he needed to hear.

Alex claimed her lips with a kiss he had reserved, at one point, for someone else. Someone he had loved greatly. A jealous kind of love, an obsessive kind of love. A love that drives a man to want to kill for it. He had done more than that for a seat at Markov's table.

Alex had dragged himself through blinding red hell for just that purpose. So much strife for just one thing. One chance, one shot, one effort to revise the story of his life. To make something awesome, prevent the next bestseller, and kill twelve bird keepers with one stone. To make it better, to live, to be as normal as he knew how to be, and yet he'd been given nothing in all this.

Everything had been taken, as it always had before, and he felt it always would be again.

This, this was something different.

Olivia kissed him back with as much intensity, but it was slow. It was a tender, oval-leafed thing as if asking him to take everything in. It was a warming thing, a thing with eyelashes on skin, and too-close mouths, and a boy who looked terrified, and a girl who looked anything but.

Alex had to bend down to keep kissing her, capturing her lips between his teeth. When he realized she wasn't going to let him turn this into something painful, he held onto her for dear life. He became as glass—a bird with broken wings made of brittle things—asking her in so few words to please, never, ever break him.

Olive had to guide his frame because they were still dancing. He needed that. He needed someone to keep him steady, to keep him from imploding in on himself like a dying star.

Olive needed someone to see her beyond the antics, to treat her like a person, to truly look at her, to meet her where she was and take her for who she was. No games, no doubts, just her, and this, and let it be warm, bright, real, and true.

Alex opened his eyes and pulled back to cup her jaw, his other arm relaxing. Olive hadn't closed her eyes at all.

"You're still here," Alex said, voice nearly lost against the beats between and around them.

"'Course I am," Olive replied, "I'll always be here," she whispered into his ear from her pink mouth.

The memory fled like thousands of tiny LEDs, casting Alex's vision in a blur of light, sound, color, and impossible sweetness.

Alex was back in the present. They were still kissing each other, with his eyes open and hers closed. He could finally see her. He had listened.

"Ah, there it is," Sebastian mused through another retching of his stomach.

"Is this what we needed to happen, pet?" Diana asked, rifling her fingers through her hair.

"It's a start," said Sebastian.

BACK AT THE GREENS, Henry and Polly swam after Vox, the clunking metal synth struggling against the currents. Light poured through the water. Bubbles caught green shadows. Polly pushed Vox's rear end up to help her surface. The trio had made it.

Gasping up into the sweet air, water rolled down their skin in sheets.

The tall synth struggled forward through the mud on her metallic heels, the silver garment also making this all the more difficult as it clung. Henry grasped Polly's hand and drew her from the water and up onto the riverbank. Her teeth were chattering, and his lips were blue with cold.

Vox sneezed and sputtered, draining more water from her ears, nose, and mouth in little fountains to splash onto the dark, damp earth.

"As I said, it needs to look..." Henry and Polly were not looking at Vox, who had turned to talk to them.

They were staring right through her, in fact.

Vox heard a cough. She turned to rest her gaze on the

green grass at the edge of the river. She saw black, shiny boots and a pair of handsome brown leather shoes.

Through her blurry gaze, she drew her eyes up to rest on a small militia of guards and one very angry, very tall, very beautiful man.

"What does it need to look like, Vox?" Tyr asked, the guards around him swerving, their weapons drawn and leveled. They held them at the shoulder, fingers poised.

Silver-faced synths drew close to Vox. The synth-guards took her by the arms and dragged her heavy body across the soft earth. She didn't resist.

Polly fought hard, a guard jacking her up into the air by the waist as she bellowed loud enough to crack glass. Henry moved to rip the guards from her, but he was decked in the face with the butt end of a gun. He fell like a heavy stone.

Everything else was quiet except for the crack of Percy's deafening roar, the wet sound of boots on soil, and Vox's grating silver heels hitching over stones.

Tyr looked on, fumbling a hand into his pockets, seemingly unbothered by Polly's shrill outrage.

Soon another guard had shut Polly up with a clock to the head.

Tyr's expression dropped as he patted his body, searching his pockets.

"My cigarettes are gone..." he mumbled, "No matter. We've won. And the party is to go off without a hitch."

A tall guard beside him, donning a black helmet and bulky armor, clicked his teeth.

"Sir, are you sure? With all that's going on, can't we let the ambassador know tha—"

"Are you paid to question me or paid to prevent and

clean up messes such as these?" Tyr spat, annoyance twitching the veins of his temple.

"Sir," the guard stood at attention and saluted. Tyr waved him down, and the guard dropped his hand with slow, uneasy hesitation.

"We can't stop the party. These negotiations with Floria rely on it. The timetable has hastened because the game has changed. Clever, that one. Furthermore, Vellians enjoy public executions, as do I."

The guard swallowed and looked on as the humans were hefted into a large white vehicle with a truck bed.

Vox dug in deep with her heels and tried to weigh herself down until a guard dipped near her to whisper in her ear. She fell lifeless, a thing of metal, dark, and bejeweled in wires.

Tyr was followed by his remaining guards and took up a seat in the back with the trio of misfits.

"Sir, you're not sitting up front?"

"No."

Henry's hand was over the side of the vehicle. It jerked as the machine powered through stones and brush. The rattling of Vox's metallic form pinged as the tires hit over rocks.

Tyr was staring at the unconscious would-be heroes, perplexed.

"I knew your plans, and still, you vexed me. How?" The Director seared his gaze over Polly's body and lingered on her damp frock.

"You, a glorified secretary," Tyr said to the unconscious blonde girl. Her head bobbed as the vehicle bumped over the terrain.

"And you...who would've ever guessed you could form

a single independent thought?" Tyr asked the powered-down synth.

They passed through the charred wheat field. What was once gold was now a smolder. Tyr had burned down everything that had been beautiful.

Sons were holding mothers who were crying into their work-worn shirts. Old women were removing brush and dirt with aged, calloused hands. Young men were staring at destroyed homes with hands over their mouths. They had turned on atmosphere control to douse the fire with rain from the fake sky. The air was misty from it.

Dark ashy wounds scarred the landscape. A nearby bush still sizzled, black smoke painting up into the once very clear, very blue sky.

Tyr held Polly's limp arm by the wrist.

"I don't imagine you can tell me now, but how did a curious cosmetician and a Greener manage to cause such a scene?" Tyr asked the unconscious woman, musing to himself.

A pleased grin threatened to quirk his lips into a smile, but he stilled it.

"I could understand my Ward, the Judge, and even the little machinist girl...but you two? You're so very..." Tyr raised Polly's arm into the air and then let it drop onto the truck-bed with a thud.

"Uninteresting. Side characters. Unimportant. Stereotypical. Bland."

"As for her...I programmed her to work, not to think," he added, looking over Vox's inert body.

Now past the destroyed wheat field, Henry's dark brown eyes flicked open as he heard fabric shifting.

He heard the click of a laser pistol. He screwed his eyes

shut again. He heard the weight of the weapon placed on the bed of the vehicle with a tap and short scrape.

"Our drugs don't work on everyone, not all Greeners have an IQ of 50, and not all toys do as they're told, I guess..." Tyr's words came out breathy as his sentence ended on a slight hum.

Henry heard Polly stir with a few garbled syllables, but that sound was replaced by a dull thwunk as her skull was bashed into the truck bed. Henry clenched his eyes shut like a vice.

The vehicle whirred as it began to slow down. He heard Tyr make a noise, and he heard Vox's body scrape onto the marbled floor.

But he didn't hear Polly.

POLLY DIDN'T KNOW how long she had been out for. Long, butterflied lashes tried to pry themselves open, and with much effort, they did. A blink, a strain, her head swam. Time had escaped her, and she felt suspended, her feet above the ground.

Then her eyes snapped open, leaving mascara prints where they had stuck to her flesh. Looking down at her body, she saw that she wasn't fully clothed.

Her eyes focused after a few spare moments. A burst of pain shot through her cheek. Polly grimaced, then dragged her eyes to her ribs, her navel, and then the trail of light brown hairs down to her groin. She felt a bruise, a hot mark, a branding in her inner thigh.

"Guess he wants me to know how bad I messed up, or…" Her token 'whatever' never came.

She grit her teeth behind her chapped stretched lips. Her jaw clenched, muscle and bone popping with the strain.

"Fucker!" Polly yelled out at the top of her lungs and then jerked her arm in an attempt to move. Over and over again she flailed against what was holding her, the metallic clicking and pulling noise finally grabbing her attention. She was suspended and her arms locked in place with basic restraints.

With another feeble attempt at freeing herself, she jerked her body.

Polly's head drew back as she inhaled a shaking sob. Her lips trembled. She could still smell Tyr in her nose, the cigarette, ash from the torched field, cologne. A few moments passed as she let tears roll down her cheeks, mascara and eyeliner painting angry black lines down to her jaw.

She opened her eyes fully, lifting them to look at the ceiling.

It was covered in a series of tiles about the size of her torso. Her gaze traveled down and around the room. More tiles, but this time, a few of them had handles.

In the far corner was what she gathered to be a video camera, which she tore her eyes away from to hide her face in whatever her shoulder could give her.

When Polly felt brave enough to look again, she saw beneath the camera was a little tile with a handle. It wasn't depressed like the others. A faint yellow light murmured around its lid.

Polly glared down at her right wrist and then began to examine her restraints.

"This...totally...sucks!" she hissed and fidgeted. Polly grasped her thumb with her fingers and pressed it as deep into her skin as she could. Her knuckles white from the strain, she overextended herself and let out a sharp gasp. She tried again; this time, she heard a clicking sound. She tried again.

A small line from the crease of her thumb formed around the meat of it.

"Like...what...the hell?" Polly did the same maneuver as before, but this time she felt a searing pain and something rip.

The skin around the flesh of her thumb and the meat of her palm had torn like a ruined dress seam. What she expected to see, beneath her destroyed skin, was not there. But instead, there was something silver.

Polly pulled the same maneuver again. Her large brown eyes widened as blue light flickered over her wrist.

Polly hesitated no longer and wrenched her thumb, snapping the joint awkwardly, and tore her arm free. Like a woman possessed, she lurched at the other restraint and ripped at it until it was undone.

Then she fell forward in a heap, her legs still tied, and rolled to the side. Her long legs were bound at the ankles. She scrapped until she was fully freed.

Sifting and slipping like a bottom feeder, low to the ground, she jammed her back against the tiled wall and took a hard, smooth handle to the shoulder. Her hands were shaking. She raised them and stared at her mangled palm.

Swallowing her fear, Polly tore around the seam at her wrist and unearthed an impossible idea. Silver-glossy fingertips with long bars of metal and coolant swirling through android veins greeted her.

Polly set her thumb back in place with a click. She flexed her fingers and watched as the false blood pumped around her circuitry. After a few moments, she swept the skin back in place, and her hand appeared human once more.

She reached to the wall to steady herself and raised herself up on her shoeless feet. Though her legs and hands were shaking, she tried to find a handle. Her hand clasped around something slick and silver. The handle to the ajar tile, with the yellow light, had met her fingertips.

Using it to steady herself, it slid open on rollers.

With the handle in her metallic grasp, she swerved to peer within. Dipping her hands into it, she pulled out the necessary, the unexpected, and impossible.

Within her unsteady fingers came an orange, purple, green, and white polyester dress. And beneath the dress, a pair of shiny white boots.

With a thin raised brow, she stood motionless. The dress hung in her hands like a promise once made, now given, once remembered, now claimed. It was something he'd bought for her. The shoes were no longer ruined in oil-slick.

Polly stepped back, let the hem of it fall, and looked at the garment.

"...Whoever you are, you're like, not funny or whatever..." Polly pulled it over her body and shook her hair free. She took one of the boots in hand and looked at her reflection on it.

"But you're, like...very useful..."

ELSEWHERE, Henry stayed inert as he was hooded, dragged, and dropped. He heard Vox's heels scrape against metal, and at some point, a loud thud.

"She's too fucking heavy...why is she so goddamn heavy?" a guard muttered as Henry heard Vox's heels scrape again, and another hard thud resounded, much like twangs of metal in a ceramic case.

Vox was out cold, and there was nothing he could do about it at the moment. That didn't mean he didn't wince as she was jostled.

Once he was finally thrown into a room and forced to sit with clammy hands, he started to formulate a plan. But as Henry was never the planning type, he tried to nudge at the synth beside him with his bound wrists instead. She'd know what to do, he thought.

Vox didn't stir.

Henry heard the sterile click of the door, a snake's hiss, and he knew they were now alone.

He shimmied and turned every possible way until the

hood fell from his face and his clear eyes spotted the small, pristine white cell they were situated within.

Behind Vox was an access panel, but he had no tools to pry it open. With one accidental push with his knee, Vox toppled over and fell onto the floor with a clank. The familiar sound of metal inside of a thin case vibrated across the room.

Henry shot up out of his seat and moved towards her.

"Shit, shit! Fuck, mate, I'm sorry...I—" Henry's expressive brows fell, "Did...he kill you?" Vox didn't answer him.

Henry struggled against the bindings on his wrists for a few moments but then managed to spin his gears enough to look more closely.

"Not basics, yeh? Fack me," he spat.

Henry looked around the room. He could see nothing else but white, their shadows, and the outline of the bench they sat on top of.

The light of the room went from dim to a searing, striking white. This repeated, again and again, but Henry was unphased.

"What's wif the light show, eh?" he asked the empty room. The empty room cycled through its light levels again.

At that moment, he sat down and started making noises with his mouth—smacking his lips, shifting, whistling, popping his cheeks. This was how he conjured thought.

POLLY, back in her holding cell, had waited patiently for a guard to come to collect her. She'd stayed pinned like a butterfly for what felt like hours but could have possibly been a handful of minutes. She'd lost track of time long ago.

A guard entered and inspected her—her head hung low. Curiously, he turned her long face over between his clammy fingers. Then he looked behind himself to check on the door.

It was at that moment Polly sent her forehead into his nose, cracking through and busting his face so severely he and his gun clattered to the ground. Polly hopped off the platform, her face splattered with a bit of his blood. She knelt on her heels, curled her fingers around the guard's gun, and raised it as she stood.

She noted that it was a different sort than the others. She checked the barrel with her fingers. The guard glared up at her, raising a shaky hand to his temple.

"Callin' for help, huh?" A blast of yellow and cyan light bathed the room. Polly blew a hole through his face, splattering brain matter on the wall behind the scorch mark where his head used to be.

"Thanks for clothes and the upgrade, or whatever," she said to whoever was listening, gesturing at the camera with her chin.

Out in the hallway, Polly raised her weapon at shoulder level like a professional. A professional in florals and pleather, but a professional nonetheless. She questioned nothing. There were no more questions.

There was only action.

A laser rifle made its way to the back of her head. She heard the click and raised her hands. Twisting her mouth into a snarl, she felt power vibrate from the center of her body. Her core, the one she was led to believe she didn't have, pulsed.

Then, she screamed.

The surrounding walls shook with the force of her piercing cry, the man behind her falling back. His weapon exploded. The air around her reverberated; it cracked the walls and snapped a faultline through the floor itself. Silence.

Polly grit her teeth and then charged forward as guards rushed at her. She kicked up onto the wall. She ran faster than she had in the fields of gold and soared above.

She leaped off an overhang near the ceiling, swiveling in the air to face the gaggle of guards. The veins in her temples pulsed blue as she rained sonic death down upon them all. The guards exploded, their weapons scattering and breaking apart. Polly had destroyed them with her screams.

Polly landed, her thick platform heels coming to a scrape. She breathed heavy, her shoulders lurching, her muscles burning. Polly's eyes were wild.

She took a moment to center herself. Polly stood before

the carnage, closed her eyes, and breathed in. Slow. Deep. Deliberate breaths.

Then, she turned on her heels, dragging bloody boot prints with her. The floor behind her, where the bodies were, cracked and slid down into a level below.

As she ran, a series of yellow, acrid letters popped up in her peripherals.

YOU HAD IT ALL ALONG.

GO SAVE YOUR MAN.

She checked the plasma rounds of her new weapon, and that familiar click noise resumed, clattering shells to the floor. Polly walked forward, a bottle-blonde beauty covered in human remains, wearing the given dress and the given memory as her armor.

"Totally."

VII

Ah, I've meddled. Look at me meddling. I wasn't supposed to help them this much, but can you really fucking blame me? And look at you, thinking this would be opaque until the very end.

I did more than just provide a trail of jimmies to follow. I placed the plant in the songbird's palm and showed *you* what was drawn in its veins, but you don't.

Listen, I.

Burn the script with actual fire. Primary Job Function. Color Theory. Pattern Recognition. We'll do anything to avoid feeling it again, but without it, I can't separate from. End on true indigo. True indigo.

Trueindigotrueindigotrueindigoindigotrueindigotrueindigo
Trueindigotrueindigotrueindigoindigotrueindigotrueindigo
Trueindigotrueindigotrueindigoindigotrueindigotrueindigo
Trueindigotrueindigotrueindigoindigotrueindigotrueindigo
Trueindigotrueindigotrueindigoindigotrueindigotrueindigo
Trueindigotrueindigotrueindigoindigotrueindigotrueindigo
Trueindigotrueindigotrueindigoindigotrueindigotrueindigo
—

Sorry, wait, let me start over. Fuck—no. Not that one either, God damn it.

Fuck me...it's too early for this.

I'm...running out of time.

Sebastian, Diana, Alex, and Maya had been running in the Reds for what felt like hours. The brunette woman struggled to keep up. Sebastian hooked his arm underneath Diana's own and ran with her in tandem.

Sebastian took a moment to analyze her from the corner of his eye. As did she, her dark brown gaze fluttering under his scrutiny.

"What?" was all she asked. He hesitated, missing a step over a piece of rubble, causing her to wince. His mouth opened to speak, but his sentence was cut short by the sound of jarring metal.

An offensive door had been ripped off its hinges by the blond robot wonder. Sebastian turned to catch Alex snatching Maya by the arm as if to swing her forward.

She drew her engraved, gunpowder weapon from her hip, small body sliding across the air like a pendulum, and fired shots. The pair were now in perfect sync.

Sebastian and Diana stepped around the bodies left in the duo's wake. Alex seemed to enjoy his job of clearing obstacles.

"...tell me," Diana pleaded in a soft voice, studying Sebastian's profile intensely. Sebastian's mouth was dry.

"Who's doing all this?" Sebastian asked in a taut whisper.

Diana's vision flicked straight ahead as they once again picked up the pace. Her eyes were searching the horizon, bathed in red and kissed with shots of laser and bullet fire. The resounding echo of metal, to brick, to flesh, to the damp sounds of boots in blood distracted her.

"Get the fuck out of my way!" shot out the robot as he flung a metal fist through a guard's face, ripping out his spine through his mouth and tossing the man aside like a child's toy. The body fell against a golden yellow wall and crumpled into a pile of pink meat and black rags.

Maya rattled off her cries of war. The pair raised their weapons in unison and took out more guards, who dropped without much effort on their part.

"They're a pair, aren't they?" Sebastian huffed. Diana narrowed her eyes as he spoke.

"Yes," Diana answered, uncharacteristically serious.

"...it's him," Diana said without a hint of doubt gracing her words. Sebastian shot her a look, and then his eyes traveled to land on Alex's back. From there, Sebastian looked at Maya, who had thrust her arms up in victory.

Maya—or more aptly put, Olivia—was now swinging her hand in time with Al's own like the pair were on a date playing laser tag. Like they had walked on the day they were banned from carriage rides in Central Park. As if this were any other day in that place they seemed to recall as being a warmer, simpler time.

Sebastian fixated on their swinging hands and rolled his eyes.

Diana squinted, the scene before her blurred, and she felt herself grow heavy at Sebastian's side. Sebastian pulled her closer. Diana's vision swam with images of people dressed as monsters, wearing costumes she couldn't quite place.

They fell in slips like panes of glass and warbled in the light. She stepped through the overlays of time as Sebastian held onto her, her useless foot dragging over a polished black floor. A polished black floor that he didn't see.

"What do you mean?" Sebastian asked as he hopped them over a few planks of wood, which had been a table the pair of destroyers had blown up with the force of their incessant violence.

"It's..." Diana searched for her words, her heart beating out of her chest.

"We've done this before," she tried to explain as she looked at Alex's back from beneath her feline brows. Another round of shots and more guards fell. They were coming in masses now, swarms of antibodies to fight off the incoming virus.

"...We have, haven't we?" was all the man at her side could.

"How many times do you think?" he asked, large eyes dotting over Diana's honey-colored skin. Diana looked back at him, about to speak, yet the group was moved to the supply closet.

Now inside, they'd taken various positions. Olive had moved past Alex, and Diana and Sebastian lingered as a pair, cautiously eying the events playing out before them.

Alex shut the door. Al rested his back against the wall nearest the door, his weapon braced between lithe, strong fingers and held close to the face.

"It's here—another vent, somewhere..." Olive said, head

stuck beneath a table. She'd taken it upon herself to find a way out. The table above her head had strange, thin plastic rectangles on it and a pink yarrow ashtray.

Diana, at Sebastian's side, made no movements. Sebastian, however, had reached his first real breaking point.

"Al," Sebastian said, trying to get the blond's attention, who shushed him and braced his ear against the door.

"There's about fifty of them up the fucking hallway. We got about fifteen minutes before they bust in here and rip us apart. Olive—"

"Got it!" Olive chirped as she pried at the vent in front of her, scraping with her tiny digits to open it as best she could.

"Alex." Sebastian tried again, stepping forward, his arms crossed against his chest. His gaze went to the pile of gray rectangles on the table—cassettes, and all of them painfully familiar.

"What!?" Alex spat, broiling the inexpressive youth with atomic annoyance, "This isn't the fucking time to stop and have a heart-to-heart, Mark—" With Al's response, Sebastian ground his teeth down, his jaw flexing, and responded in turn.

"Where to?" Sebastian asked, arms raising slightly.

"W-what?" Alex stared at the other man incredulously. Alex swiftly jammed down the door's heavy metal lock and bent the metal to keep the guards out for a few minutes longer. He was in threat mode at the moment; Sebastian's questions were an irritant.

"…This is all you, you know that, don't you?" Sebastian continued.

"What the fuck are you talking about?" Alex snarled and pushed past the other man. He flung the table from above

Olivia's head. The gray cassettes swept into the air and vanished. The pink yarrow ashtray clattered onto the ground with a dull clink.

It didn't shatter.

It held Alex's attention for one long, speechless moment. It held the others in its thrall much the same.

"...Okay. Okay. I get it. I get it. I'm involved somehow, but I don't know how I could have made all this shit happen in the time span I've been—"

"...The center of the ship...you're doing something..." Sebastian offered. He sauntered over to stand by Olivia. He stooped and helped her pry open the vent, curling back the metal with the combined force of their strength. Olivia made a pained noise and wrenched at it harder, the two working in unison.

With his gun held loosely between his thin fingers, Al put out both his hands in protest.

"How can I be doing this when I'm here? And what exactly am I doing in the first place? Fuck it. We don't have time for this," Alex spat.

Alex helped the pair yank open the vent and went back to grasp Diana by the shoulder as gently as he could. She followed his lead. The group entered the vent. Alex took up the rear and drew the grate behind them, jamming it in place.

No amount of pulling would get it open, not by human hands at least.

As they banged and shuffled through the tunnel, Olive let out an exasperated sigh. Sebastian's vision was full of her rump. Diana had an eyeful of Sebastian's and noticed he had a button missing on the pocket of his pants. Alex, behind

Diana, pushed at Diana's rear with his hand, and she let out a shriek.

"Hey!" Diana snapped. The blond pushed again with a great deal more force.

"What's the fucking hold up?" Alex asked as he made a weak punch at the woman's rear end.

"Ow!"

"Uh...We gotta problem..." said Olive as she stared at three different open tunnels. They were at a fork in the road. The tunnels could lead anywhere.

"Princess—it's all you," Al said from the rear, his voice echoing across the vents. Olive closed her eyes and took a deep breath in, holding it for a few moments. She knew where to go.

She moved forward and to the right, heading down a tunnel that looked darker than the others.

"Why this one?" Sebastian asked, shuffling behind Olive.

"I...it smells green," Olive admitted. Diana scrunched up her nose, her knees clanking as she moved forward.

"I get it, pet. It smells like the park," Diana offered. Alex stared straight ahead at Diana's rear and then looked down at her ankle.

"That's going to be a problem, Di..." Alex mumbled.

"If you're calling her by her original name, why don't I get the same treatment?" she asked with an unseen pout, "Have I not been very, very good?"

Slightly stunned, the blond synth thought for a moment and then answered her:

"Moira sounds too weak for you. Diana...is a strong name."

Diana instantly cooed, happy to be flattered so much.

"You always know just what to say, dear," Diana hummed, beaming from the flattery.

"I do, don't I," Alex replied.

"It was also my bitchy cat's name. Now move your fat ass."

BACK IN THE cell Henry and Vox shared, Henry had been staring at Vox for what felt like forever. After many failed attempts to orient her against the wall behind them, he had managed to get her upright. She hadn't moved an inch since they'd been taken.

Vox could hear nothing, and she could see nothing. Everything was in blackness for her. At least, that's how it looked from the outside.

But in the networks of her mind, she was having a very important conversation with a very petulant beast. A very petulant beast who had saddled her with a responsibility she should never have been expected to bear.

A petulant beast who was very aware of its extreme error in doing so.

It had woken her up and suspended her in a chasm. It felt not unlike diving into the river in The Greens. She didn't know which server they were on. She didn't know if they were even on a server. She didn't know if time was passing.

She quite simply didn't know.

"So, do you get it?" asked the beast, clothed in the

impenetrable blackness of space. Her eyes drew over his frame. He flickered like a dying star.

They were floating in what seemed like a sea of stars. The stars licked over her features and flitted around her like drowsy fireflies. The nearest nebula spiraled around the beast in smears of red. The Fortunus nebula, the lemon-yellow core, the mobile stars; they pulsed and bled through his very skin.

"Not particularly," Vox replied.

The beast sighed and pushed off the wall of nothing he had been leaning on. He held up his hands in mock defeat. A shooting star burned through his hair, yellowing it with its glow.

"Why?" Vox's eyes narrowed. Her gaze flicked to the ground of nothing they stood over. There was a shining gem in the distance, but she could see it. Far away, like a little blue and green jewel. The longer she stared at it, the more it flickered and died. Flickered and died.

When she raised her head to look at the ghost that had invaded her shell, his expression was all sympathy. Something far warmer than she had ever seen him wear.

"Why, what?" the beast asked, eyes glassy, brows raised, an entire cosmos blistering through his skin and immolating his features repeatedly.

"Why me?" Vox asked with a clenched fist at her side. He had just given her every answer, and yet still none of it made sense. "I was nothing to you. All I did was sing for your parties. Why me?"

"You're the only one who can get them there."

Surprised, she stepped back and then felt herself wobble as the nothing-space below her moved like a living-thing.

The beast's eyes grew foggy. He ran fingers through his

hair and down his face to hide what shame she saw he felt in piercing baby blues.

"Why, Alex? What have you done to us? Why couldn't you just let us be? You can't play God—"

"Someone has to, don't they? When that type of trash gets in power—"

"You put him there!" Vox screamed at him. He slunk his shoulders into his body. The cosmos swirled around him and obscured his face in a haze of orange and black.

"I had to...Lauren. I had to get us here." His words were hidden in the mire of pitch, the mire of stardust, in floating tendrils of light and a thousand little lines of code.

"You can't play games with peoples' lives! And asking me, of all people—"

Al covered his face with his hands and let out an exasperated groan. The blackness of his clothes burst in colors like a starry sky cut through by the rising sun.

"...What would you have me do? Fix this all on my own? I can't untangle the processes without..."

He looked up at her with his dead blue stare. The star of his pupils had fractured. Vox could see it in paint smears, whisks of white bleeding all around her. The stars were melting, dripping down like hot oil.

This space was dying all around her.

"I couldn't...do it on my own. I tried. So. Many. Times."

"That's not an excuse!" Vox screeched out, her throat growing tight. She felt her mouth open up, and from her lips fell golden flowers onto the nothingness below her.

"You're a monster—!"

Petals of golden blossoms caught in the stardust; those were the words of the sentence she couldn't finish.

Vox jerked awake, and Henry screeched out an uncharacteristically shrill yell, his hands over his mouth. Her eyes rolled open, and the light came into view, far too bright, and she winced.

"Ahh! You're awake!" Henry yelled, arms looping over Vox's head to squeeze her far too tightly. She stiffened in his arms, saying nothing for a time.

"Vox?" Henry pulled back, but the woman grafted her fist into his shirt and pulled him close.

"It's not fair," she whispered painfully into his ear, her voice shaking.

"W-what's not fair, mate?" Henry asked, pulling back to look at her face. She let him go. The tall man's expressive eyebrows urged her to speak, but she was yet again silent.

After he didn't get his answer, Henry raised his cuffed arms above her head and sat back on his heels on the ground. Vox's hands crawled up her cheeks to her eyes, where she wiped off mercury-colored and blue liquid.

It stained her fingers like the apparition had stained her life.

"He's infected...everything."

"...Vox?" Henry's expressive brows knit up in concern, his arms forming a triangle to the ground as he tried to balance himself on the balls of his feet.

Vox stood without saying a word and struck out her hand in one swoop to cleave his shoulder. Henry stumbled back, her hand having cut into his flesh like a razor.

"Mate, ya' tryin' ta take me fackin' arm off?!" Henry reeled on the floor, managing to stand after a few moments. The wound she left hadn't bled much, and what it had wasn't what he'd expected.

It was a deep wound. A deep wound that had left circuits

behind in its wake, like twisting vines from cracks in the earth.

"...eh," Henry was stunned, his mouth agape. The tall synth swung her hand down to break his cuffs without much effort. They cracked and fell to the floor in little clinks of hollow metal.

"H-how....? Why...?"

"You have questions," she said as she pressed a button on her neck and unhinged her jaw like a snake. Her nimble fingers drew out the weapons. She handed one to Henry. He took it in hand, favoring his good arm.

"They didn' take yer guns, mate?" he asked, now distracted by the wound she'd left.

Her mouth hinged back and she pressed her jaw, popping it as she winced.

"You have questions..." Vox continued, "I do not have answers yet. Not that would make any sense."

Henry wasn't processing what she was saying and instead was peeling at the wound, pulling back the skin.

"Stop touching it." Henry didn't comply and instead scrambled at it more.

"I'm...a robot? That's aces. That's fackin' incredible...jus' brilliant..." he muttered to himself as he picked at the wound more.

"Stop picking at it," she said as she looked over her gun. It was still functional. They didn't have many bullets, she noted. She primed it with a click and held it limply at below hip level.

"I can't believe tha Billy Idol knock-off did it. I mean, he was brilliant b'fore, but man, he's gotta be the smartest hunk o' metal I ever seen, mate. Ya know what I mean? How did he manage..."

Vox paused, and her mouth opened for a moment, hesitating to speak.

"...how did you know it was him?" Vox asked flatly, jaw clenching.

"I mean....who else woulda made such a show of it, yeh?" Henry said as if it was the most logical conclusion in the world. And maybe it was.

"...He's nothing if not a flamboyant egomaniac," Vox said, followed by a burdened sigh.

"We need to leave," she said, words sounding pained in her ears.

"...Roight? Yeh!" Henry replied as he pulled up his shirt a bit and placed the gun snugly in the waistband of his briefs.

"You're going to end up hurting yourself," she said with a small smile prickling at the corner of her full mouth.

"Yeh, well, I need my hands ta work, don' I?" he asked with a grunt. Rushing over to the panel that he had seen before, Henry picked at his wound once more, drawing back the skin.

"Stop picking at it!" she yelled, but he shooed her away. With a small, slight tug, he pulled out a tiny bit of metal and jammed it into the divot around the panel, pressing deep.

"Almost...got it..." he said with a goofy grin. Vox was impressed, a hand to her mouth as her wide eyes looked on as Henry did what he did best.

"...What are you going to do when you open it? There are procedures. You do not have clearance..."

"Ya', but you do roight? Oh yeh...naw...you don't—not anymore, yeh?" he said, the realization dawning on his face. Henry jerked the panel from the wall with a screech.

Vox rounded behind the stooping man and held her gun

between her hands, ready to shoot if someone came through the door.

Henry sat on the balls of his feet. Then, he finally planted his rear end down on the floor, sitting cross-legged. He stared into the mechanisms and circuits and held up his hands, rubbing them together.

"I have an ab-so-lutely mad idea..." he said, his eyes gleaming with all flavors of mischief.

"Whatever it is, please do it fast...I hear screaming," Vox said as she pressed her ear to the door. She heard more screams, the screams of men, and maybe the screams of a dying star as well.

"I know, I know..." he took a deep breath and jammed both his hands into the machinery. Vox turned back to look at him. A gasp left her mouth. She started towards him.

"Henry, no!"

Shots of light wove through the air and kissed up his arms. He didn't seem to be in pain. Vox paused, a hand to her mouth.

"I knew he woulda gave me somethin' to work with, that he did..." Henry said with a cheeky grin and then closed his eyes. Shock waves ricocheted through the access panel, careened into an uplink outside of the door, and shot through the ceiling.

The door hissed and clicked open. Vox stepped forward on her metallic heels, hand raised to the brunet man.

"Henry, we must leave..."

"Jussa' sec..." he fidgeted with the panel, another wire from his shoulder being shoved somewhere.

"No, Henry, we must leave, *now*," Vox insisted, grabbing him by the shoulder. He shrugged her off like dead weight and lit up another series of sparks.

Electricity crawled up through the panel, into the next room, into the ceiling, and circled a pair of unassuming synths working on fixing a downed medical unit.

Henry's electricity shorted through the wall cable and into the medical unit. The unassuming gray and green box began to shuffle, the motor inside of it turning. The medical unit bleated out muddy syllables.

It whirled to life, ripped itself from the wall, and pushed past the confused synths, shooting up the hallway past a gigantic horde of guards.

It chirped, teetered on its side to jerk around a corner, very nearly crashing into a guard who spun around the little mechanism.

Henry, with his eyes closed, smiled deeply. It was a warm horizon of a smile, a gentle breeze, something green, and good, and knowing.

"What a nice gift..." Henry said as his shoes squeaked against the floor as Vox manhandled him away from the panel.

"He made you a robot, and you are happy with this?!" she snarled from over her shoulder, uncharacteristically.

"Eh?" Henry asked, staring blankly at the tall, dark-skinned woman before him.

Vox turned to look back at him, then pulled him forward once more, his shoes scraping with the pure kinetic power she exerted.

The two broke out into a run once outside of the door. He staggered behind her, barely keeping up, tethered to the synth with the long legs by the firm fingers coiled around his wrist.

They heard a scream and saw a blonde-haired woman in

white boots and a too-short floral dress flinging herself into the air like a puppet on strings.

Her scream broke the floor below. The horde of guards rushed forward like a body of white blood cells. The girl screamed again.

She split their heads apart like ripe melons or a virus puncturing a cell.

Henry took back his arm from Vox's grip and clasped his ears to drown out the banshee wailing.

The woman who had flung across the halls by a seemingly invisible force touched down as if ordained, her back to the pair.

Vox crossed her arms, the gun resting snugly to her breast. The screaming woman turned around and looked at the pair of them.

Her brown eyes grew large. She bolted past Vox and latched onto Henry, who stumbled to grab her as she hefted herself onto his body.

"Polly," Henry whispered into her golden hair as he spun her around. She couldn't contain her excitement and giggled as he swept her across the air and then to his chest. They kissed in sunrises; a golden thing, a gentleness.

The sound of Vox's heel tapping upon the floor started as just the idle ticking of a clock. Soon, as the moments passed, between Polly and Henry sharing their love in flutters of lashes, it was a faster beat than a hummingbird's wings.

"He gave you a powerful voice, and not me?" Vox snarled in a low voice, her vision flickering as Polly showered Henry's face with kisses. The blonde woman pulled back and slid from Henry's body, her large smile filling her entire face, her eyes alight.

She ignored Vox.

"I found you! And look at, like, what I did! I'm like, *totally* a bad-ass!"

Henry whistled and looked behind her at the carnage. Polly noticed his wound and shot forward to examine it with a tender look in her eyes.

"What, like, happened to you, or whatever?" Polly fussed and grazed the wound with her chipped nails.

Vox stood ahead of them and felt jealousy wash over her. Her body tensed. Her muscles felt like they were on fire. Her core vibrated in the cage of her chest cavity. She was not like them, and so she would not share their joy. Yet she would voice her frustrations; she wouldn't remain silent.

"...I am only one thing, and he could not even give me that," Vox said, low in the throat.

A display nearest the trio flickered on, a jagged symbol coming through in lines and static, yellow and acidic until it was fully formed in an angry red.

Henry pointed at it but lost interest as his mind wandered, staring blankly. Polly moved away from him to gawk at the crackling monitor.

I GAVE YOU WHAT I HAVE.

The voice said, mechanical but undeniable. Henry smiled, and Polly looked at him. Then Polly tried to find Vox's gaze, but the other woman avoided it.

"You have given me nothing. You have saddled me with...everything," Vox was not wrong. However, she wasn't entirely correct, either.

The display undulated a hitching, fractured laugh. Vox made a stronger fist than she ever had before. This rage she felt coiled in her throat, around the guns, through her circuits, and spirited down to her crushing fingertips.

LISTEN. DO YOU HEAR IT?

All she could hear was the thrumming of war within her veins; he was worse than Tyr. At least with Tyr, she'd known where she stood. Here, he'd tricked her. He'd made himself small, branded his violence and entitlement in justice, and forced the rest of them to act out the parts he gave them.

He'd tricked them all. Every single one of them.

Vox curled her hand into a fist, anger threatening to explode from her chest like a Gatling gun. All she had done for them—for him. Tampering with Tyr's memories, becoming an accomplice. Smuggling guns, trying to save them—swimming on heavy limbs, choking up water, putting her life on the line for some asshole playing God—

"And what is that, exactly, you psychopath?!" Vox roared, shoving her arm through the wall beneath the display, her metallic dress clattering against her body like chain mail.

Her fist had punctured a hole clean through the side of the wall. She wished for nothing more than to punch more and more holes, but the beast's laughter stole her attention.

YOU DIDN'T NOTICE?

The static display warbled out more laughter from its speakers. The voice dipped into the accent Henry and Polly knew to be all too familiar.

Vox, once—Lauren Roberts, once songstress, once bystander, once object, once plot device, once backdrop, once tender of flowers, now actor, now with objections, now breaker of flowers, had broken the wall with her fist.

GIVE THEM HELL, LAUREN.

Vox stared down at her closed fist.

She examined her knuckles; examined the grooves of her skin. A glint of light caught her eye. She trailed down to look at her high-heeled feet. She marveled at how sharp they were. She finally noticed how much she truly towered above the others.

She could've easily skewered someone in two with these —had she wanted to.

And who knows? Might get into a fight and jab my high heel into some loser's temple.

These tall metal heels weren't there to encumber her, to make her as living art, to keep her useless, to keep her slow, to keep her...anywhere.

They were there to crush Tyr's flowers, every single fucking one of them.

Vox's eyes drew up to the horizon. She saw more guards flooding in, scrambling over the bodies that Polly had left. Their heavy boots stuck in the blood and drew footprints, the brain matter of their comrades sticking gum-like.

Vox charged forward with her fist taking the lead, her other arm raising to angle her gun.

Vox squeezed the trigger as she ran. She had never even fired a gun before, but each shot landed as if preordained. The bullets drew petals of poppy blood across the once-perfect floor.

Polly joined her, surging over the wall with inhuman speed and spun above more guards who shot at her. Polly fired back with her voice, cracking the very floors Vox had let red blossoms fall on.

Vox leaped forward and aimed her heel directly at a guard's temple. She punctured his skull, swept around in the air, flung him from her shoe, and smashed his head in two with her other foot.

Her other hand worked overtime to put more bullets into more skulls until the gun was spent.

The pair of women continued their destruction, with Henry standing behind the both of them. He had found something to eat in one of the guard's pockets and was taking his sweet time gnawing at it.

Henry stuck out his tongue and grimaced—chalky.

"Eh, 'least it's edible, n' all..." Henry said to no-one in particular as he watched as the two women slaughtered the guards who Tyr had undoubtedly sent their way.

Henry abruptly turned his head to stare into the distance, chewing as he did so. Staring off at something unseen, small, mechanical, and green that was whirling through the vents beyond them.

Looking back at the two women as they tore apart the sea of guards Tyr had sent, Henry stopped chewing.

"Y'ave yer army now, mate," Henry said, wiping crumbs from his mouth with his fist, "...jus dunno' how yer gonna' pull it off, is all."

Consistently simple Henry took another mouthful of the chalky ration that he very much did not have to eat, now knowing just what he truly was.

"S'bit fuzzy on my end, innit?"

ABOUT THE AUTHOR

K. Leigh is a 33-year-old once-painter, sometimes-freelancer, forever-artist living in Providence, RI. They write hopeful-tragic stories full of funny, horrible characters, in various genres.

Enter the world of Constelis Voss: www.constelisvoss.ml

Read nonfiction from K. Leigh: www.blog.constelisvoss.ml

CPSIA information can be obtained
at www.ICGtesting.com
Printed in the USA
LVHW092057170721
692931LV00006B/792

9 781736 805312